BARRY E WOODHAM

STAR SEED

AWAKENING

The collective has spread its seed across the interstellar void and found intelligence. Can the high king and his allies stop it from conquering all life in the multiverse?

BARRY E WOODHAM

STAR SEED
AWAKENING

The collective has spread its seed across the interstellar void
and found intelligence. Can the high king and his allies stop it
from conquering all life in the multiverse?

MEREO
Cirencester

Mereo Books

1A The Wool Market Dyer Street Cirencester Gloucestershire GL7 2PR
An imprint of Memoirs Publishing www.mereobooks.com

Star-Seed Awakening: 978-1-86151-217-8

First published in Great Britain in 2014
by Mereo Books, an imprint of Memoirs Publishing

Copyright ©2014

Barry E Woodham has asserted his right under the Copyright Designs and Patents
Act 1988 to be identified as the author of this work.

The address for Memoirs Publishing Group Limited can be found at www.memoirspublishing.com

The Memoirs Publishing Group Ltd Reg. No. 7834348

The Memoirs Publishing Group supports both The Forest Stewardship Council® (FSC®) and the PEFC®
leading international forest-certification organisations. Our books carrying both the FSC label and the PEFC®
and are printed on FSC®-certified paper. FSC® is the only forest-certification scheme supported by the leading
environmental organisations including Greenpeace. Our paper procurement policy can be found at
www.memoirspublishing.com/environment

Cover Design - Ray Lipscombe

Typeset in 11.5/15pt Garamond
by Wiltshire Associates Publisher Services Ltd. Printed and bound in Great Britain by Printondemand-
Worldwide, Peterborough PE2 6XD

ABOUT THE AUTHOR

Barry Woodham was born in 1943 and has lived in Swindon, Wiltshire in England all of his life. He is married with three sons all in their forties and lives happily in retirement with his wife Janet (48 good years & more to come!) He spent his working life as a design engineer/draughtsman and worked on the nuclear fusion project for thirteen years.

Finding himself with nothing to read one lunchtime, he began to write the saga of the Gnathe and the Genesis Project. The thought occurred to him that any life form evolved to live in this world would not be able to cope with the micro-organisms of another eco-system on an alien planet. After many of his colleagues began to read the chapters as quickly as he could finish them he continued on and finished the first book. The alien Gnathe are instinctive genetic engineers and alter living creatures to be their tools by the use of their brooding pouches controlled by the third sex. This first book was set millions of years after the sun has entered its red giant stage and is set on a vastly altered Jupiter. Humanity and intelligent Panchimpanzees are recreated by four Guardians made of nanotechnology sent towards the stars from the dying Earth, to bring back mankind. One ship is stuck in the Kuiper Belt until it begins to fall towards the new sun and the crew are activated.

Barry was able to take early retirement through a legacy and continued to write the next book following on from *Genesis*

2, The Genesis Debt. These have both been self-published on Amazon under the title *The Genesis Debt*. Recently he decided to put all 15 years' worth of writing in the hands of a new publisher and spend some of his sons' inheritance!

While writing *Genesis Weapon* he decided to link all the books together as The Genesis Project and work all the books into a series. The fourth, *The Genesis Search*, was set hundreds of thousands of years after the events that occurred in *Genesis Weapon*. This part of the saga concerns the deliberate collision of the Andromeda Galaxy with ours in the distant future. What kind of entity could cause this to happen and why? This book attempts to settle those questions and concerns building a hunter/killer group from the ones who defeated the Goss in Book Three by going back in time to remove their DNA and clone them, restoring their stored minds into young healthy bodies. At the same time whole solar systems are being rebuilt and moved by wormhole technology to the other side of our galaxy to be launched as a globular cluster towards the Large Magellanic Cloud and safety.

Whilst writing this fourth book the idea came to Barry that the group of mixed human and aliens would find themselves having to deal with the abandoned machine intelligence of von Neumann probes left behind by the events produced by the 'Harvester' and this became the basis of the fifth Book, *Genesis 3*, A New Beginning.

He then considered what would happen after this universe runs down, and how to build a new one to take its place. The Elf War followed and as so many were asking if he could go back to the Elf world, he did so, and Molock's Wand was the result. Now the trilogy has been completed with Star-Seed Awakening.

I hope that you will enjoy reading these books as much as all the others and as much as I have enjoyed writing them.

Barry E. Woodham

barry.e.woodham@btinternet.com

THE GENESIS PROJECT

Book 1 - Genesis 2

Book 2 - The Genesis Debt

Book 3 – Genesis Weapon

Book 4 - The Genesis Search

Book 5 - Genesis 3 - A New Beginning

THE ELF-WAR TRILOGY

Book 1- The Elf War

Book 2 - Molock's Wand

Book 3 – Star-Seed Awakening

Tales of the Ferryman can be read on Barry's blog, http://sci-fiauthor.blogspot.co.uk

CHAPTER ONE

The Tree was hundreds of millions of years old and it measured over two miles high and half a mile wide at the base. It was the only one of its kind on this world, and it now dominated the landscape for a hundred miles in every direction. In the beginning it had grown from a seedling in the shade of other plants, located on a vast plain with mountain ranges thrusting into the sky at the edges. Now all living things grew in its shade. Over the years, it had withstood earthquake, storms and drought, but now it faced the final catastrophe.

Tectonic plates had danced the dance of over and under many times, but now pressure deep beneath the Tree was beginning to build. A ball of magma was forming far beneath the roots. Over the last million years the caldera had begun to push up the land around the tree. It was a slow push, as these things take time. Eventually the magma began to form a resurgent dome. Over hundreds of thousands of years, the Tree began to feel the tilt as the land rose and the edges of the caldera rose with it. The tree was now on the brow of a low hill in the middle of the place where the volcano would form. In a few hundred thousand years the whole of this area would cease to exist, as a supervolcano would blow the whole fertile plain across thousands of square miles.

Before the tilt became excessive and forced the tree to fall, it came to a decision; not that it could think, but its instincts enabled it to choose the best course for survival. Accepting that there was nothing it could do to stop this natural phenomenon, it put out as many flowers as it could, without losing its tenacious grip on the soil. For the first time in the several hundred million years since its growth had begun, a sweet odour filled the air as flower after flower opened. The tree channelled nutrients high up to its topmost branches to feed them.

The first animals to reach the Tree were flying creatures that struggled to reach the nectar hidden in the base of each flower. Many of them remained stuck fast, trapped by the sticky syrup, and in their thrashing about they died, their bodies fertilising the flowers and becoming absorbed into the nutrients. From the plains and hills came climbing creatures that headed for the tree, all of them overcome by a desire for the sweet sticky nectar that dribbled out of the flowers. For countless millennia the Tree had poisoned all that had attempted to climb or nest in the branches. Now it needed those life-forms to reproduce. Many of them died trying, and their bodies helped to feed the Tree by decaying around its trunk. As the flowers shed their petals and the seed-cases formed, once more the Tree poisoned every creature that dared to climb or fly onto its branches.

The tilt of the land was beginning to throw excessive strain on the roots of the Tree as its top moved further and further from the perpendicular. It directed branches to dive down and root into the ground to support the strain on the tilted side. Now the creation of its seeds could take place, but the most important part of the plan was the seed-case. The blueprint for the seed-case was carried in the genetic coding of the Tree and was billions of years old.

Steadily the Tree wove the protective fabric of its craft around the precious cargo that would lie slumbering for eons before a fertile place could be found. The seed-cases would detach themselves from the Tree and begin to climb towards the top when finished. If they touched each other, they climbed together for a while, all heading for the topmost branches two miles from the ground. These were changing shape and being re-absorbed into the trunk. Now a new structure began to form as a mushroom shape flared out from the central stem, waiting for the advent of the climbing seed-cases.

The designer of the seed-cases had imported many minerals that would be necessary to the final stage of the seeds' destination. The tree had invested thousands of years of root search to bring minerals and heavy metals to the surface and pass them upwards to the fertilised flowers that had produced the seed-cases. Now the Tree began the process that would lead to its destruction.

The root system expanded into those poisonous areas which it had purposely avoided, seeking out the heavy metals it needed for its ultimate plan. Amongst these metallic salts were fragments of uranium 234, and these the Tree wrapped in lead, to prevent an early reaction. At the same time it began a growth spurt half way up its miles-high trunk and deposited certain of the metallic ores to expand outwards to produce a bell-like shape. The centre of the trunk still pushed nutrients into the upper regions following the construction of the seed-cases. Here it stored volatile substances in strengthened containers and fitted them to the sides of its creation. Metals and vegetable compounds joined together to produce different skins, each with a different purpose which would be realised in the far future.

A quarter of the way up from the roots, the Tree constructed a place to store the enriched uranium in lead shrouds. This became a cankerous gall, the holding place for the radiating fuel that would propel the upper part of the Tree to a sub-orbital position after ignition. That was when the next part of the plan would take place. Once the seed-cases had started their journey to the top of the tree, the Tree began the next part of the plan in earnest.

Lead had been wrapped around the uranium so that the radiation would not poison the seed-cases and corrupt the seeds. Now the branches that were no longer of any use began to be shed by the tree. Leaves were grown larger and modified to become stabilising wings as those branches warped themselves back towards the trunk. The topmost branches had developed into a bell-shaped structure into which the seed-cases tucked themselves. Once they were safely in position, they were held tightly in place by the bell constricting around them.

Now the Tree needed to put the next part of the design into action. A mile and a half below this giant seedpod, rapid changes began to take place. A larger bell of metal was created above the ignition chamber, fanning out to compress the shockwave and hurl the remains of the Tree into sub-orbital position.

All traces of uranium were husbanded together and kept in two separate piles so that a slow ignition did not take place. The metal accumulated in non-critical sections until enough had been refined by the seed-cases to be ready. Now the radiation was beginning to build and the two masses were becoming hot.

There was no time to rest. Carefully the Tree thinned the material that kept the two semi-critical masses apart. The heat generated now dissolved the barriers and the two were slammed together by the fabric of the Tree and became one. The fireball filled the lower bell as the trunk disintegrated, hurling the seed-pod-bearing tree high into the air. It rode the shockwave in front of the heat. The downward thrust opened up the volcano beneath it.

The atomic explosion threw the seedpod into sub-orbit,

guided by its wings, which kept it stable. It rose like a giant dart far above the last vestiges of air. Now the bell-shaped seed-pod carrier ruptured and peeled apart, ejecting the seed-cases away from the star that had warmed the Tree that gave it life, casting the seed-cases far and wide.

Once the seed-cases had scattered, secondary propulsion units fired up and projected the hundreds of thousands of seed-cases into many different vectors and out into interstellar space. Now their journeys would begin, as each independent 'craft' would attempt to leave this star system behind and seek a new and fertile world.

Far below, the Tree was consumed by the atomic fire that it had carefully gathered as tiny fragments of uranium were explosively brought together. The shock-wave awoke the sleeping giant underneath, where the Tree had rooted. The ball of magma exploded through the now much thinned crust and threw the remains of the Tree after the first stage, which had gone as far as it could. It gathered up the remains of the trunk, turning most of it to ash, and began to return to earth.

The explosion coated the continent with a pyroclastic flow that ignited all in its path. A twenty-five mile high ash cloud erupted into the sky and the air tuned dark. The world below became trapped in a nightfall which would last for centuries. Everything within a hundred-mile radius of the eruption was destroyed as ten thousand cubic meters of land was tossed into the air. This ash in the atmosphere would lower global temperatures by 20°C, dropping the planet into an ice age and depositing a layer of ash ten feet thick for a thousand miles around.

The tree died, content that it had spread its unique form of life into the cosmos. Its servants died with it.

Once the fuel had been exhausted, the seed-cases

disengaged from the empty propulsion units and left them behind. Now they spread solar sails to catch the stellar wind and gained speed to attain escape velocity from the star of their birth. Those cases that were facing towards the sun ultimately perished in its fires. Those that faced away began the long journey out of the reach of the star. Several gas giants lay between the planet of their birth and the outer reaches. Hundreds of the seed-cases perished, drawn into the gravity wells of these planets, and some landed on airless moons, failing to germinate; they would remain in this state of suspended readiness for ever. There was nothing here for the children of the tree, and the survivors carried on into the great darkness beyond the last outposts orbiting the star.

Several million years later, a seed-case began the long drop towards a new sun, passing through a Kuiper belt of frozen balls of gas and stony residue. Enough starlight was captured by the sensors to waken the systems that made sure that the seed-case did not collide with any frozen planetoids. It would be many thousands of years before the sensors would pick up the traces that would mean a water-world. Once that happened, the seed-case would alter course to put it in orbit around the chosen world.

As it got closer, slowly the warmth of the new sun began to have an effect upon the seed-case and new vegetal circuits triggered off new responses. Long-stored growth cells activated, and leaves used liquid water to expand into vanes so that a sycamore seed shape began to form. A tiny drop of water was jetted to the side to give the seed-case a slow spin. Now each vane was periodically bathed in sunlight, and while the water liquefied the wing grew further in the increasing warmth of the star. As the vane rotated into shadow, the wing froze. The new wings would slow the passage through the atmosphere to prevent it from burning up. The tree had planned for every contingency that its originator had passed down. Its best hope for the optimum survival of the seed was to engage with a host.

That host was getting closer by the moment. The Leader of the raptors operating the ship had willed her Spellbinder away from the gravitational pull of the parallel Earth to investigate a strange incoming object that had shown up on the sensors. She was a new type of velociraptor, a triumph of genetic engineering by the elfin scientists; not only were her senses sharper than many that had gone before, she had opposable thumbs. She had been named by the Halfling John Smith as Vinr-Margr, meaning Leader of many. Her potential was off the scale, and she was hatched in the certainty that she would one day rule the council of raptors by her wisdom. At the moment she was simply called Vinr, not yet having earned the second part of her name.

She sat perched in the command chair that had formed around her when she had taken command. Her tail lay in the groove provided, feathers tucked in, while her taloned feet dug into the elf-stone at the base of the chair. Her staff of power was thrust into the operation pit linking her to the Spellbinder's mind. This mind was a composite of other raptors that had sat this chair before her and linked to this was a copy of the human, John Smith, which took the dominant position among other non-raptor minds. She had access to the knowledge of goblin artificers, elfin scientists and a link to the High King himself, if he was ever needed.

Vinr called upon all of these as she studied the object steadily approaching the planet which lay beneath them, another Earth in a parallel universe. She could sense metallic salts forged into bizarre patterns that passed through the strange thing which was well hidden inside. It was alive in the sense that it was in a form of suspended animation that was giving way to awakening. Dotted along its sides were receptors that drank and processed the starlight the object received, as it slowly spun on its axis. It clearly had purpose and had been fashioned by an intelligent source.

"What do you make of it, Spellbinder? All of our joined senses believe that this thing is vegetable in content," Vinr thought.

The human/elf John Smith agreed and added, "I sense that there is not enough metal inside that thing for it to be a manufactured item."

Goblin minds made observations and agreed.

The composite mind of the Spellbinder interrupted the many conversations flowing to and fro with the statement, "I have plotted its trajectory back as far as I can. The object has come from well outside. This thing has travelled from another star to get here. Judging by its speed it may have been travelling for many millions of years, yet it is potentially alive. There is movement on the skin as portals open and close. It is absorbing energy from the star and storing it somewhere inside. We have no experience with a life-form such as this. Yes, this is unquestionably a life-form of some kind and not an engineered machine."

Vinr considered that thought by calling upon the mind of the Halfling scientist and engineer. "Well, John Smith, what do you advise? Your race has a scientific background and had generations of your kind delving into things that you did not understand. How dangerous do you think it is?"

"That I cannot answer for sure," the swift response came into her mind. "One thing is apparent and that is, the closer it gets to this star, the more alive it becomes. It has a purpose. I have scanned the area behind the object and it is alone. There are no more of its kind following on behind. We have never come into contact with any life-form of this kind in any of the parallel universes that we have visited via the Rifts. This is totally new. What remains to be seen is whether this thing could be a threat to our civilization. I am torn between taking it on board and dissecting it to see just what it is or following the object to see what it will do."

The velociraptor thought about the situation and came to a decision.

"Spellbinder, match our trajectory with this thing and follow it to its destination. We will observe what it does without any interference. This world is many Rifts away from our home-base and whatever happens here will not affect us. On this Earth the asteroid never hit the planet and the evolutionary path has been very different for the last sixty-five million years. This is a dinosaur world in which no mammals rose to ascendancy. Our own type of dinosaur developed beyond the primitive state of our long past and they are using tools and fire. They live in groups and co-operate, so we deem them worthy of contact in the future. We will be observers. We will wait and see what this object becomes when it reaches the planet below."

The seed-case was aware of the presence of the Spellbinder, but it did not register the elf vessel as a threat. The guidance system was locked onto the planet that was coming into range. It had already looked at the fourth planet from the star and rejected it in favour of this one. Sensors registered the existence of water in liquid and solid states. It also became aware of the electrochemical signatures of many different life-forms. This too was important to the seed-case, and it planned accordingly. The all-important seeds would be modified to take this into account.

The first kiss of the outer fringes of atmosphere began to

be felt by the wings of the seed-case as they began to slow its interplanetary journey. This triggered the wings to allow braking edges to project from them and dip the leading edge of the case deeper into the increasingly thick air. The first layer of the roughened husk began to burn off, leaving a shiny metallic skin underneath it. Now the nose pushed upwards and the streamlined shape hidden underneath the outer husk began to show. The seed-case began a ducks-and-drakes manoeuvre to skip in and out of the atmosphere, losing speed and height over and over again until the only direction was downwards. Now a simple glide through a white-hot fireball began, and no reversal of purpose was possible.

The fireball disintegrated the hard metal skin surrounding the precious cargo and once more attacked the new husk underneath it. From this layer new wings sprang out of recessed holding spaces and once again applied a braking force. Now the seed-case trajectory became a long glide as it passed over a vast sea, heading for a large continent that had been picked out as having great promise for the next stage of the mission.

At thirty thousand feet the seed-case came apart and scattered sycamore key-shaped seed-carriers into the turbulent air. They spun and scattered across the continent below until they hit three thousand feet, when they ruptured, spilling hundreds of thousands of dandelion-shaped seeds. Now the next stage of the mission began as the seeds danced and spread in the winds, each searching for a host to root in.

Vinr changed the Spellbinder's shape to a glider and applied braking vanes to slow it down so that they could follow the seed-case down to the planet's surface. When the seed-case came apart, scattering the smaller carriers, the raptor applied more flaps, to slow down even more. The whirling sycamore key-shaped seed-cases spread outwards like an expanding cloud. Vinr was taken completely by surprise when they came apart again and released thousands of dandelion-type seeds from each carrier, each the size of a human's fist. Now the Spellbinder was enveloped in a candyfloss cloud that was rapidly left behind, scattering on the winds.

The Spellbinder spoke to Vinr. "The dispersal pattern will mean that almost the whole of this continent will be touched by a seed."

The human, John Smith's copied mind, insisted, "We must stay for a while and watch to see how this life-form develops. All eventualities seem to have been considered to ensure maximum survival. I think we should land and take some time here and watch its development. We were fortunate to be here at the arrival of this interstellar visitor. It is a new form of life, totally different to anything we have encountered before. This is an amazing chance to study it and to see what your distant cousins make of it."

Vinr agreed. She sent the Spellbinder into a slow descent, aiming for a flat space away from the vast swamp that stretched for miles down to the sea and became part of an estuary. She extended four legs from the main body of the sentient ship and formed wide pads on the bottom of them. The rest of the Spellbinder she altered to a globular shape and set the scanners to constantly sweep the area to see if there was any change. The plains were covered in a fern forest which was grazed by beasts similar to those that wandered the plains of Scion on Haven. Some of them were quite as large as the brachiosaurus that herded and fed on the edges of the swamplands near her home. This world was quite wild however, with little sign of any cultivation.

One of the scanners caught a drifting seed and followed it through the air as it was carried towards one of the long-necked beasts. The combined intelligence of the Spellbinder watched fascinated as the fist-sized seed floated down onto the back of the creature. It burrowed into the flesh of the enormous beast without it noticing. Some time passed. The sauropod continued to feed on the ferns without any change until it suddenly raised its head and looked around. The creature now examined the area where it was standing in some detail. Others of its kind responded in the same fashion. More, smaller beasts came out of the undergrowth and stared around. Some of them, with large eyes, climbed up the legs of the sauropod and onto its back and stood staring at the countryside around them. Several of them still had seed stems projecting from their heads, with the ball of candyfloss catching the breeze. These velociraptors were the ones with bigger brains, the tool users that could have been cousins to the crew of the Spellbinder. They were carnivores and hunted in packs. They also built shelters to fend off other predators, using fire as a deterrent. Now their behaviour was undergoing a strange change.

Vinr and her crew looked through the sensors of the Spellbinder at the strange events that were happening wherever they could see. The many different life-forms were all now subjected to an alien purpose. The giant sauropods began to gravitate together until they stood in a circle, heads to the centre and tails to the outside. This pattern was repeated all over the plains, as far as the Spellbinder could apply its sensors. The animals then began a strange dance, lifting their forelegs up and slamming them down in a rhythmic pattern, then adding the back legs in a matching pattern. The pulse could be felt inside the Spellbinder, indeed inside the bodies of the flesh-and-blood crew.

"Spellbinder, what is going on? I can feel the vibration going right into my bones," Vinr said. She grasped hold of the command chair as the entire ship swayed with the motion of the ground.

The ship's mind considered the situation and suddenly realised what was going on.

"Vinr, I think I know what is happening" it said. "The area is being seismically mapped. Whatever has surfaced in the life-forms that the seeds have touched has co-ordinated together. I think there is a group mind out there that has a purpose of its own. This is a totally alien form of life. We have never contacted anything like it before. We also have a problem that needs thinking about."

"What problem, Spellbinder?"

"I can feel that I myself have been invaded by hundreds of the organism's seeds. Until I can think of a way of removing all of them, we dare not go home and risk taking this organism with us. We need to stay here and study it, and find out how we can control it if necessary."

CHAPTER TWO

The seeds of the Tree studied the results of the seismic disturbance. It was becoming more aware of itself as time went by. Old memories began to surface of its origins and the millions of years it had spent growing on its host world, preparing it for ejection into interstellar space. The positions of the tectonic plates began to take shape in its mind, and the edges became fully defined. These were the areas to be avoided, as they corresponded to volcanic action. Tree-seeds had fallen from coast to coast right across the continent, so the composite mind began to construct a map of its new territory. It was searching for rivers flowing through deep soil and large lakes situated across the plains.

The sense of identity grew with every passing moment, until slowly the Collective was reborn. The more hosts it inhabited, the greater its mental capacity grew, but as it expanded, it became aware of another identity greater than itself. This could not be drawn into its web. Nevertheless, seeds had penetrated into this unknown substance and something came back from this contact. Its parent had used whatever life-forms were available to it on the previous world, but they were very primitive in relation to the ones it had absorbed on this virgin planet. It remembered its past life spent in a static mode watching the seasons pass. It wondered how its other clones had fared, and whether any of them had reached a world as suitable as this. Awareness came to the mind that was now spread over this sea-locked continent. There were many things it needed to do to ensure the next part of its cycle would take place.

It released its control on the giant sauropods and allowed them to feed on the vegetation around them. As it assessed the meat-carrying capacity of these behemoths, it decided to terminate some of the very elderly ones to feed the growing packs of hungry predators. For these creatures a time of plenty would dawn. A balance would be maintained between those meat-eaters that showed promise of increased intelligence and the less worthy ones, which would now serve as carrion-eaters.

The Collective became very interested in the tool-using velociraptors, as nothing so advanced had evolved on its previous world. They would give it a far greater control over its new home than had been possible before, but the anomaly remained of the other independent intelligence it had made contact with. Was this a competitor? So far the burrowing seeds had not been able to exert any control over the 'other' and had remained in a semi-dormant state.

Vinr was aware through the sensor system of her living ship that 'passengers' had made it into the Spellbinder's skin. These were being studied by the composite minds that made up the 'personality' of the Spellbinder. The nannite construction of the Elf-stone gave an advantage against the invader, in that it could and did weave an impenetrable shield around each seed. John Smith's inquiring mind directed the goblins within his direction to take apart one of the seeds and study its DNA. They found keys set inside the helix which would lock onto 'alien' DNA and convert it to blend with the intruder. The organism was a co-option of other species. It was a blend of animal protein and vegetation the like of which the scientific minds of the Spellbinder had never seen before. It was the most dangerous and insidious living entity they had ever encountered. They had no idea what it would become.

Vinr considered the information flowing into her receptive mind and made her decision. Until they had resolved just what threat, if any, was posed by this organism which had travelled interstellar space to get here, there could be no going back to Peterkin's Kingdom. It was not yet the time to extend the Spellbinder's abilities to try and make contact with the High King until she knew more. There were many facets to the Spellbinder's mind, and she could call upon any of them for advice if she so wished. She had become used to the multiple identities blended into her ship and had learned to shut them out at will. This had been done at Haven by skilled elfin psychologists who had spent a lot of time training her before she was given a Spellbinder of her own. Her people, the 'Folk', had been deeply honoured by her achievements and had proudly waited for her to pick her crew.

She had picked ten of the best bred raptors, taking three males and seven females with her. Vinr was a 'Leader of Ten' and was gravid with a clutch of eggs, having mated with all three males. It would be these raptors that would incubate the eggs when they were laid, as all males did.

Using the techniques the elves had shown her, she gave out a broadcast to all members of the Spellbinder. "We must stay here and study this organism until we can be sure that we can leave without taking any of this life-form back with us" she told them. "I cannot tell you how long we will be here, only that we cannot leave until we are sure. Whatever has landed on this world seems to have all of the larger life-forms under its control. The composite minds of our ship cannot determine just what the creature is. All I can tell you is that what we followed into insertion was not made by any animal; it was grown."

CHAPTER TWO

The rest of the crew accepted Vinr's command without question and connected themselves to the sensor network of the Spellbinder. Some of them examined the degree of penetration of the seeds into the nannite elf-stone to check the depth. Some scanned the creatures gathered around the Spellbinder's base, while others monitored events further away. One thing became obvious, and that was the degree of obedience radiating around the countryside. All the larger forms of life selected by being implanted by the 'seeds' had a purpose that dictated their lives.

Vinr's feathers drooped as she sat desperately trying to think what to do about the situation. They were a multi-dimensional distance from the Haven Rift, having travelled far from one Rift to another in their search for another dinosaur planet. She was not a telepathic adept like the senior elves who had trained her. She could draw upon the added power of the Spellbinder to aid her, but was uncertain just how far her call for help would carry. Several Rifts from here there was an ice world that she knew the goblins were interested in studying and they had hailed each other, as their respective ships had passed. There was a good chance that the survey expedition might still be there.

"Spellbinder!"

"Yes, Vinr," the composite mind answered.

"I need to speak with the goblin contingent," the raptor said.

Swelling up from his position came the mind of Beedle Leaf-shredder, who had been a scientist and strong telepath in his former existence. Now he was part of the Spellbinder Collective.

"What can I do for you, my lady?" he asked.

"I need you to blend your mind with mine and reach out to the goblin expedition to the ice world we passed several Rifts ago. Can you do this?"

"I think I can, but I may need extra life energy to do so. You carry new life inside you as unborn eggs," the goblin replied. "I may need to draw on that life energy to be able to reach that far. Have I your permission to do this?"

Vinr was horrified at the sacrifice she would have to give, but agreed. She gripped the staff of power and drew on the abilities of the goblin minds backing up Beedle and generating the push. She felt herself reach out from her flesh and out of the Spellbinder's fabric as the goblins pushed her consciousness away from this planet and through the first Rift. She threaded her way through several Rifts, feeling the life drain from some of her eggs, as her life energy was not quite enough to take her where she needed to go.

Contact was made!

A goblin-based Spellbinder picked up her questing mind and asked, "What do you want, little one?"

"I need help here" she replied. We have stumbled onto a great threat to all of our lives. Come here, but do not land. You must stay in orbit while I explain. I must go!"

Vinr came back to her body, feeling the loss of the eggs that had been sacrificed to give her that extra life energy to carry out her mission.

Beedle's mind entered hers and said, "You did well young one. You could not yourself spare the life that was needed. There will be other eggs to carry on your line. Not all are dead. Now would be the time to release them and wait until the Goblin Spellbinder gets here. You will be able to explain to them quite easily from here to orbit what we have found. Also we may know more about what this creature could do to us."

Vinr nodded and felt the first movements in her ovipositor as events caught up with her and she made her way towards the nest that the males had made for her. Third-male was waiting for her with fresh meat to give her added strength while she strained and pushed. As she chewed and swallowed the bloody morsels, she wondered how many of her children had been sacrificed to power that cry for help.

As always an odd number of eggs were laid and nine fresh ones were arranged in amongst the plucked out feathers which all the males had donated. Third-male climbed on, settled over them and rolled them around his feet. It might take several days before she could be sure which ones would be addled. It would take three weeks until the shells cracked and she could see if her breeding would ring true. Any of the offspring without opposable thumbs would have their necks broken and be discarded. Those she would eat still warm. One thing the elves had impressed on her was that genetic purity was the only path that the raptors could take or risk dropping back to a previous genetic milestone.

She looked around for First Male and Second-male to see what they were engaged in studying. Vinr linked minds with the other fathers of her eggs to find that they were attempting to dig out the growths that had burrowed into the Spellbinder. They had merged minds with the Spellbinder and were trying to ease away the elf-stone from the embedded seeds. At each opportunity, the seeds burrowed deeper.

Vinr fed herself into the gestalt and gave the command, "Stop! All you are doing is opening up the substance of the Spellbinder and allowing the seeds to get further into our vessel. Instead of trying to dig them out, crush them one by one by constricting the elf-stone around them. Harden the area in touch with each seed first. Spend some time trying that while I try to reach out to the goblin vessel."

Before she could try that, however, she needed more information about what was going on outside. This time she ignored the efforts of First Male and Second-male, connecting to the Spellbinder directly.

"Show me what is going on outside, Spellbinder. John Smith, give me your attention," she ordered, and sat once more in the command chair.

The copy of the mind of the High King's main scientific colleague answered, "Vinr, see through my eyes and sensors."

She sat and marvelled at the level of obedience and co-operation that became apparent between the dinosaurs, which were moving purposefully. A few of the huge sauropods had dropped onto their sides and died. Meat-eaters were taking their place and eating sufficient to satisfy their needs. In between the big killers were the smaller raptors, which were cutting away at the carcasses and harvesting the meat. This was being taken back to the shelters that the raptors had built. As she watched, a large, rouge, T Rex-type meat-eater lumbered into view, heading for the carrion on show. Massing about nine tons and extending to forty feet long, it was confident in its supremacy and totally without fear. This animal was obviously not under control and was intent on one thing; fresh meat.

When the creature dipped its head to take a first bite, one of the raptors ran up its back and thrust a seed into the beast's neck, where it burrowed out of view. The theropod suddenly shuddered, then withdrew its bloody head out of the cavity and looked around. It took no notice of the raptor that had seeded it and merely dipped its head again and continued to feed.

Vinr shivered. "That huge creature was subdued in seconds, John Smith," she said. "We have no defence over that kind of domination. Apart from staying here I just don't know what to do."

"Wait, Leader of Ten. Wait until the goblin ship arrives and I can transfer all of my data so that it can be studied at Haven. Peterkin has to have all the information that we can give him before he can act. In the meantime I will harden my own surface, so that no more seeds can get a purchase. I have managed to squash some of them, but not enough to be sure that we could ever be seed-free."

"Then wait. We must and gather as much information about this life-form that we can," concluded Vinr.

Over the next few days the Spellbinder and its crew continued to monitor the baffling events that took place 'outside' and recorded them. An entire day was spent sustaining investigating 'attacks' by large flying pterosaurs similar to the Quetzalcoatlus that flew the skies of Haven and Alfheimr. Wingspans the size of gliders and hooked claws capable of lifting a raptor in one foot scrabbled for purchase on the hull. Whatever was controlling them continued to use them to dive-bomb the globe that was mounted on top of the four legs. The Spellbinder merely hardened the outer surfaces and allowed the rain to wash off the resulting bloodstains, as beast after beast died trying to crack it open. After a while this fruitless series of attacks finished and the flying creatures were abandoned by the controlling intelligence. The Spellbinder kept the surfaces opaque from the outside the vessel, but transparent from inside. Night and day the area around the ship was watched continually by the raptors and the sentient vessel.

"Vinr! Wake this instant," cried Five of Ten, and shook her by her upper arm. Leader of Ten ruffled her feathers around her neck and stretched out both arms. As sleep rapidly disappeared she swung her needle-sharp teeth round at the intruder by instinct and snapped her jaws shut just shy of Five of Ten's face.

"What is it?" she asked, as Five of Ten danced out of reach.

"The sauropods are on the move, Vinr. They are grouping around the Spellbinder's feet. I think they are going to try toppling the Spellbinder by pressing around the legs. What shall we do?"

"Arm all of the crew with the AK-47s we brought with us and fire through the walls into the beasts, but only aim for the joints" Vinr ordered. "That size of beast will just absorb the bullets and they will be wasted. Use only what ammunition clips will do the job. Remember that what we have is limited until the goblin ship arrives. They can drop more ammunition from orbit on top of our Spellbinder, in a carrier made of Elf-stone, so that the material is at the same frequency as ours. If it is done quickly then none of the seeds will penetrate our defences." Vinr broke open the arms locker.

All the members of the crew made their ways down into the legs of the Spellbinder except for Second-male, who was taking his turn sitting the eggs. The walls of the Spellbinder had gone transparent and the sauropods could be seen ponderously making their way towards the legs of the Spellbinder.

Vinr opened her mind to the crew and ordered, "Aim for the knees at this distance and make a barrier of their bodies if you can. Measured bursts at both front legs. Do not keep your fingers on the triggers and wasted ammunition."

The first bursts of fire did the trick, as knees that were not evolved for this pressure came apart, tipping the huge beasts onto their bellies and chests. The ground shook with the weight of the giant dinosaurs as they toppled over. Soon there was a wall of meat around the legs of the Spellbinder, preventing any more of the sauropods from approaching the legs. The outsides of the leg walls were diamond hard, but from the inside they were penetrable and the bullets could get out, though the seeds could not get in. Vinr fumed at Peterkin's insistence that the automatic rifles supplied were the extent of the weaponry that he would allow the spellbinders to carry.

He had also restricted the amount of ammunition clips stocked on board.

The High King's attitude was that the Spellbinders were not to become weapons of war and would be minimally armed. This would ensure that peaceful solutions would be found to any problems the exploring Spellbinders might encounter. He had also restricted the Spellbinders' powers to manipulate time, as this too could lead to military solutions as well as a restriction on size. The Spellbinders were still capable of shape-changing, but could no longer become huge umbrellas that could dominate hundreds of square miles underneath. Peterkin's Spellbinder, however, retained all the original systems and was the only one of its kind.

Vinr was left wishing that she had those resources at her disposal now, to rid her vessel of the many parasitic seeds embedded in the hull. She checked the clips of ammunition left over and felt a twinge of worry at the amount that was left. There were bullets left in the magazine of her AK-47, but only enough for another burst.

She opened her mind to the others and asked, "What have you got left?"

They reported that there was enough for several more incidents.

"Hold your positions here while I go back to the command chair and find out if our back-up has arrived," Vinr commanded. She quickly made her way out of the leg and into the main control area and sank into her chair. Leader of Ten thrust her command staff into the socket and asked, "Spellbinder, do we have contact yet with the goblin ship?"

"I sense a disturbance in the orbital paths above us," the Spellbinder told her. "It is indeed Chisbolt Hungry-jaw and his family. I am relaying all of our information to their memory banks as we speak."

Vinr opened her mind to the goblin ship and greeted the goblin. "Chis! I'm in trouble down here. I need every clip of bullets you possess. We are besieged by every living thing of any size down here. We dare not lift into orbit as we are infested with the seeds that exploded from the seed-case we foolishly followed down. The last thing we tried was using the giant sauropods to topple us over. We shot out their knee-caps and they dropped to form a barrier of meat that will keep the rest at bay. It will take some time before they rot away or are consumed by the carrion eaters. The awful thing is that there are folk of our kind that could be cousins to our species. It is obvious that they are being controlled by whatever has entered their bodies. It would be very wrong to abandon these people to certain servitude."

"Sounds like you're in the shit my young friend, well and truly!" replied Chisbolt. "This is what we will do. I will send down my son, Nuzac, in a piece of my Spellbinder so that he can match molecular patterns with yours and enter your ship without taking any of these accursed seeds with him." He paused and thought for a moment, then went on, "He will carry down all the ammunition clips we have on board and his own AK in case you need another one. I will travel as fast as I can back to Haven and ask the High King what to do. Somehow I think he will get involved. You have stumbled onto a life-form that is unique among all the universes, and looking at the information you have passed onto our Spellbinder, it is one of the most dangerous."

"I believe you're right" said Vinr. "We saw a seed take possession of one of the big meat-eaters in a few moments. It changed its behaviour completely and you could sense it thinking. The scary thing about it is that all the life-forms are linked together as one organism. Everything that has been touched by a seed is part of a greater co-operation. We have no idea what the final game will be or what it will do next."

"OK. Nuzac is on his way to you as we speak. It should not take more than a few minutes for him to dart his way into the top of your Spellbinder. Activate to receive him.

Far above the grounded Spellbinder, a piece of the goblin ship changed shape and dropped out of orbit. Nuzac was completely surrounded by elf-stone except for his head, which had a globe surrounding it with a built-in air supply. His arms became wings and his feet the controlling tail directing the angle of penetration through the atmosphere. There could be no return. The ammunition clips were strapped to his body and his own AK-47 secured under his belly. The rate of descent was slow enough not to bake him in situ, but fast enough to give him manoeuvrability. Just to make sure, the two Spellbinders fed him the controlling flexes of arms and feet to direct him towards the Raptors' ship. He had a few moments to see the situation underneath him as he glimpsed the circle of dead or dying sauropods surrounding the marooned Spellbinder.

The back of his sky-plane suddenly erupted into a giant dandelion seed to slow him down, with just enough distance to drop him safely onto the top of the Raptors' vessel. He merged into the hull and was deposited into the control chamber. His spindly body bowed under the weight of the ammunition he was carrying along with his own rifle.

Vinr leapt from her chair to catch the goblin as he buckled at his knees. She quickly undid the straps holding the clips and they fell to the floor, where First-male quickly picked them up and stacked them away.

Nuzac straightened up, cupped Vinr's needle-toothed jaw in his green, skinny hand and asked, "What deep shit have you got yourself into now, my young friend?"

Vinr stared back at her friend's large dark eyes with the long eyelashes she lacked and replied, "That's the problem, my hatching companion, we don't quite know. Merge with our Spellbinder and you will know as much as we do".

The goblin cocked his head to one side and said, "Spellbinder open up your memory banks and let me speak with Beedle Leaf-shredder".

The copied mind of the goblin's distant relative surfaced from the gestalt and spoke, "Greetings, great-nephew. You have been very hasty in your decision to come here, but your family were always a little too well-endowed with bravery."

"Uncle, what have you found out about the situation here? Fill my mind," the goblin replied. He stood, examined the information and pulled at the tufts of hair growing from inside his pointed ears as he assimilated the knowledge.

Nuzac turned to Vinr and said, "Sit in the chair my young friend and tell my father to get to Haven as fast as he can. We are going to need a lot more experience, weapons and authority before we do anything here. Whatever has landed on this world has every large life-form on this continent under its control. How it did so is beyond our knowledge. Even your John Smith with his human attributes has no answers to give. No, young raptor, we must sit here and wait for the High King to come. We will do nothing without his say-so."

Vinr sat in the chair and grasped the staff of power. She linked with the goblin ship in orbit high above her and relayed the instructions that Nuzac had given her. It never occurred to her to question the goblin, as he was the first contact she had had with the world as she hatched. He was twenty times older than she was and had always been there at instruction times to teach her to think outside her species.

High above her, Chisbolt Hungry-jaw and his family turned the Spellbinder into the next Rift and were on their way home to Haven, leaving the raptors grounded on the parallel Earth.

There they would have to stay and wait for Peterkin's arrival. Even that might not be enough to lift them from the domination of the life-form that had claimed a world for its own.

CHAPTER THREE

The carcasses of the sauropods had begun to rot over the weeks they had lain in the sun and rain. Many of the big meat-eaters moved in and steadily fed on the remains. There were no disputes amongst them, or fighting. Outside the air was thick with flies, the smell of the carrion having drawn them for miles. Gradually the walls of meat began to diminish as they were turned into vast piles of excrement. Safe inside the diamond-hard walls of the Spellbinder the crew of raptors kept a wary eye on events outside.

Vinr was waiting for the eggs that had remained alive to crack. Four of them had died within her; the mind of Beedle had warned her that some would have to be sacrificed to feed the mental push required to penetrate the Rifts. Now First Male had signalled that those eggs that remained alive were ready to hatch. He climbed off the nest of feathers and waited with Vinr and the other raptors who were not engaged in watching outside to see what would transpire. Cracks began to appear as new life pushed against the shells to burst into the world. One was a little in front of the others and a snout broke through, followed by two spindly arms. The chick rolled out and stood on unsteady legs, looking around at the faces staring into the nest.

Vinr leaned in and held up a morsel of raw meat above the chick's jaws. It reached up, snapped the bloody chunk from Vinr's fingers and sat down to swallow it.

"That one has opposable thumbs. Keep it," she said and watched as one by one the other eggs split open.

First Male picked out a slightly smaller chick and said, "No thumbs".

"Eat it," Vinr commanded, and reached in to another chick to check its tiny three-fingered hands. She put it to one side with a portion of meat, then reached for another and put it with the first two. Second Male reached in and took another chick and held it up to show Vinr.

"This one is good and she is strong!"

The goblin watched dispassionately as the raptors sorted the clutch and weeded out any of the young without opposable thumbs. He fully understood that the genetic variation that the elves had introduced to the raptors was prized beyond measure. The tool-using capabilities of the velociraptors which had thumbs took them far up the evolutionary ladder. The species were ruthless in its culling and would not allow any chick to pass on its defective genes, so they were sorted at hatching time.

Nuzac had been there when Vinr had broken out of her egg-shell and had been allowed to feed her from birth. She was genetically modified to have increased intelligence as well as her thumbs. That extra hook in the DNA that altered the brain to receive and send thoughts to other intelligent creatures had been fixed in her mother and grandmother. It had bred true, and Vinr had been allocated to him to educate him and to teach him to think in a manner other than the other raptors. He had watched her grow and had treated her as if she was his own daughter - and he had plenty of those. His father had also taken a hand in the education of the young protégée in handling the multi-mind that each Spellbinder carried. Chisbolt Hungry-jaw had admitted her to his extended family and made her a part of his life.

Nuzac placed a hand on the raptor's feathery ruff around her neck and leaned forward.

"Well you have four young that meet the standard. Let us hope that we will raise them on the community worlds and not here," insisted Nuzac. "I have tried every trick that I can think of using the Spellbinder to rid us of the seeds embedded in the walls and failed. We can't shed them or crush them, so until we have inspired help, this is where we will be staying. I have no idea what the controlling mind out there has in store for us in the near future, so I suggest that we walk away from here and find a safer place to stop and wait."

Vinr looked round at her friend and mentor and said, "It's worth a try. I'm sure we can uproot ourselves from here and at least go to where we can get some fresh water."

She handed the chick she was holding to Second Female and made her way to the command chair.

"Spellbinder!" she said. "I think it best if we walk away from the edge of this swamp and head for a more elevated position near to some accessible fresh water."

"I have the area around us mapped out. There is a rocky plateau some miles to the East of here which we can reach with very little trouble. A waterfall runs into a basin there which is meltwater from a glacier hundreds of miles from here," the intelligence replied.

All eyes of the Collective watched as the strange object began to remove its legs from the swampy ground and slowly walked away. It still could not make out if this unresponsive thing was a threat or not. It felt that anything not under its control would drop into that category, but was undecided what to do at this moment. It decided to wait and find out what the thing would do next. So far it had not threatened the Collective, just defended itself. There was still very much to do before the Quickening took place. There was a whole continent to survey before the final choice was made, and there was this other impenetrable life-form to study.

The object's ability to move had caught the Collective's attention and had been a great surprise. It had tried all kinds of actions to gain entrance and had failed. This strange object had followed the seed-case down to the fertile ground, but had done nothing as yet to try and wrest away the dominance that the Collective required to carry out its purpose. The seeds embedded in the skin of the creature sent back confusing signals. Some had been destroyed, but the others had burrowed deep into the object, though they had not 'joined' with the living thing they had penetrated.

It watched through hundreds of eyes as the ball-shaped creature made its steady way across the swampy ground onto the beginning of an upthrust mantle of rock. To the Collective's amazement it began to climb the hillside until it found a water source and settled down by adjusting the legs to form a stable platform. One of the legs anchored itself in the middle of a stream, while the others bit into the hard rock face of the plateau and bedded into the rock. There was no chance that the Collective could send more of the giant beasts to topple this object over, as they could not climb the steep slope it was anchored on. The one thing that registered in the Collective's growing mind was that whatever this thing was, it needed water. That gave it a possible leverage against this potential adversary.

The Collective had lived on many worlds and had used the life-forms to do its bidding over and over again. It had never come across intelligent creatures on any world it had dominated. The tool-using creatures on this world were the first it had encountered. They were going to be extremely useful to it during the expansion stage of its conquest.

New thoughts filled its consciousness that had not been so

intense in its past lives. It even wondered how its other clones had fared after the parent tree had blasted the seed-cases out of the cradle of the last planet. It had never given them a thought in the past, and this higher plane of thought was new. For far too long its nature had been dominated by the use of inferior life-forms, and to plant its roots into fertile soil and grow was enough. This mind was fresh, and far greater in magnitude than those that had gone before it. It discovered that it now had ambitions that transcended the Quickening, although that would come in the end, as it always did. It now possessed the emotion of curiosity; something that it had not had before.

The Spellbinder took on fresh water through a sieve so fine that no micro-organisms could enter into the sentient vessel. It filled the tanks it had hastily formed. Now they needed meat to add to the dehydrated rations they had brought with them. This would mean that they would have to go outside.

Nuzac spoke to the Spellbinder. "Build an armoured suit for myself and Vinr so that we can go outside without being seeded" he said.

The two of them were soon covered in a candy-floss cloud of green elf-stone which spread from the floor rapidly upwards. A transparent globe formed over both of their heads fitted with air filters, allowing them to breathe the air outside.

Vinr and Nuzac both checked that their AKs were loaded and that they had a spare clip each. Vinr opened her mind to the other raptors and said, "Keep a tight watch all around the two of us. Any meaningful behaviour that is seen, tell us immediately. Be our eyes and ears."

With that the two friends sank through the floor, slid down one of the legs and stepped onto the stony ground.

"The herds are down the bottom of the slope and the other side of the trees," the goblin remarked. "Gun cocked? Ready?"

"Yes, old friend, but who leads? I think maybe it should be me, as I at least look to be of the same life-form as everything else," the raptor replied and made her way down the slope. As she went, she paid out a thin, super-strong thread that connected back to the Spellbinder. The feeling of being watched intensified as they walked into the light undergrowth that started as soon as they walked off the rocky ground. There was a small herd of iguanodon feeding on a lush tree they had pushed over, and they were busily stripping the green leaves from the branches.

Nuzac stopped dead and connected to the mind of the raptor. "Go for the youngest one and we can get back to the Spellbinder" he said.

Vinr gave a snort of irritation at being guided in hunting by her goblin friend, and all heads came up to watch the advance of the two. She quickly aimed at the chest of the smallest and watched it drop to a single shot. The loud bang of the rifle panicked the others, and they swung away and stampeded away through the trees and bushes; all except one of them, which stood its ground and stared at them.

The Spellbinder quickly advised them to hitch onto the cable and retreat back to the shelter of the ship. As Vinr strode forward, the iguanodon did not give ground. It just stood there watching the actions of the two hunters. The raptor wrapped the cable around a back leg of the dead dinosaur and it bonded to itself. The Spellbinder rapidly reeled the cable in and the creature was soon on its way back to the vessel. As they retreated, the lone iguanodon walked slowly back with them and showed no fear at all as it watched everything that the goblin and the velociraptor did. It struggled somewhat with the increased angle of the slope back to the Spellbinder, but it continued to climb until the way became impossible for an animal its size to continue.

The carcass of the iguanodon was hauled up into the belly of the ship and disappeared from sight. Then the two hunters made their way back to the leg they had travelled down from the main body of the Spellbinder.

Before they had quite got to safety a warning was given by Five of Ten. "Look out to your left! There are six of the folk making their way towards you. All of them are armed with spears. They are not making any attempt to be hidden from you. They want to be seen."

Vinr and Nuzac turned and watched as the raptors indigenous to this world walked slowly into view and laid their weapons down on the ground. They were very similar to the crew of the Spellbinder. They had crests of feathers on their heads and ruffs around their necks, with the same rigid, feathered tail. There were large 'flight' feathers running down both arms which could be extended to help turn and twist when in pursuit of prey. The patterns on the feathers were bands of grey and dark grey which gave them a camouflage effect, particularly when they stood in shadow.

One of them began to whistle and chirrup to Vinr, ignoring the goblin by her side. The noises being made by the raptor were almost understandable and very similar to Vinr's own language, which the crew spoke on board the Spellbinder. Try as she might, Vinr could make little sense of it, except when now and again some kind of meaning slipped through. She felt that she and Nuzac were not being threatened by these people, but saying that, they seemed to want something. One of them stepped forward from the group and offered them an unattached seed. Then it pointed to Vinr's head.

"They are inviting you to become one of them" said the goblin. "Don't do it, Vinr! You have no idea what touching that seed could do to you. Remember how quick the big meat-eater was taken over."

"OK, I have no intention of doing anything like that, but cover me anyway. I am going to try and make contact with the one who spoke to me by getting into her thoughts. I am not sure if she can cope with mind-to-mind contact, so be ready for any sudden movements towards us. I will get the Spellbinder to drop a shield in front of us first."

The Spellbinder immediately extended a wall from the leg of the vessel so that it made a barrier between them. The raptors watched without fear as a light-green translucent wall formed about the two creatures facing them.

Vinr settled her mind and opened the link to the raptor that had tried to communicate with her. She was overcome with the emotion of fear and of being trapped. Pictures of family life surfaced for a few moments and of eggs nurtured in a communal nest tended by males. Then a different sense of purpose was imposed over the lives of the people of the swamp's edge. All this came from what seemed to be a mind so controlled that it had little will of its own.

Vinr reached deeper and found to her surprise the mind she reached was nothing like a raptor's mind, or anything else that she had contacted before. This mind was vast, and incredibly old.

She formed the concept of "Who, what?"

The answer came, "I am the Collective. You will now serve me, as do these creatures until the time of the Quickening."

"We will not!" retorted Vinr. "We are free of domination and wish to remain so. We serve no-one but our own kind and we co-operate with many species for the common good."

"You are not of this world!" the Collective replied. Then it began to probe Vinr's memories. Vinr closed up her mind as the elves had taught her and put a shield in front of her uppermost thoughts. The Collective became a hot spike in her mind, and she reached out to the Spellbinder for strength and help.

The Collective was relentless and began to question the raptor. "This thing by your side. What is it? Are there many more of them?"

Against her will information began to seep out from underneath her shield, and the Spellbinder closed the psychic link down. Nuzac hauled the limp frame of the raptor back inside the Spellbinder's leg and the two of them rose up to the command centre.

When the link was cut, Vinr began to vomit in reaction to the questioning by the alien being. She emptied her stomach onto the floor, and the Spellbinder absorbed the mess as quickly as it was deposited. The pain in her head was intense, but through it she had glimpsed odd pieces of history lived by the Collectives mind. What she had, she fed to the Spellbinder to analyse and make sense of.

Outside the vessel, the group of raptors still remained where they had been left by their new master. Vinr's crew had examined the dead iguanodon using the sensors of the Spellbinder, to make sure there was nothing inside it that might spread the contamination. They found nothing, so they had the animal butchered into joints and mince to be stored and kept cool. All of the crew would benefit by eating fresh meat that evening. There were still dehydrated stores on board that could be reconstructed into palliative meals, but these remained in store as emergency rations.

Nuzac gripped the raptor by her shoulders and said, "That was nasty! What did it do with you? I was completely cut off from the link you made with that thing. I was shut out! That might mean that it can only deal with one telepathic wavelength at a time."

"Had that raptor touched me with the seed that it was carrying, I'm sure that I would have become one of the Collective's slaves" replied Vinr. "The power of the mind I touched was greater than anything you can imagine. Each of them has a seed connected with its neural system. It has blended with the raptors' bodies in such a way as to become part of them. Whatever that thing is, it is now part of every life-form a seed has touched."

"Those seeds fell over almost the whole of this continent. That means we are dealing with a life-form of colossal size," the goblin gasped. "It can watch us through a hundred thousand eyes. The thing is, what does it want?"

"That I could not understand at all. The concept was so alien that I just could not get my mind around it. The one thing I am sure of is that it will not tolerate competition. It wants us to join its collective consciousness and become part of it. There is one other thing I gleaned - it understands that we are not from here. That is a new thought that it has to deal with. If we dare to go outside again, I'm sure we will be attacked and attempts will be made to seed us."

Nuzac twined a finger through his ear tufts and stared at his dinosaurian friend. "In here we stay and wait for reinforcements to come" he said. "We will have to make the meat last as long as we can. After that it's reconstituted freeze-dried pap. I don't think we will get away with another hunting jaunt."

Outside, the Collective sorted through the memories of the similar, tool-using creature it had dominated. There was much here that it could not understand. This was the first really intelligent life-form it had encountered on the many worlds it had dominated. The ones it had taken over on this world were exceedingly useful and had added their intelligence to the Collective to an immense degree. The new one that it had fleetingly touched was off the scale, compared with the ones it had dominated here.

Furthermore, the being that had stood next to the creature

was totally different from any life-form on this world. It could speak with its mind to the other creature that thought of itself as leader of a specified number of its own kind. It was in the memories. This was also a new thing to be considered. The very concept of 'Leader' was new.

Voluntary co-operation between different intelligent creatures was also new. Bits and pieces of Vinr's memories came to light and the Collective found that there was a society of many different intelligent creatures all living in harmony. This concept was very new. For the first time in its cloned life the Collective felt the emotion of unease as it continued to try to understand the fragments of memory harvested in the brief contact. There was also the exceedingly strong mind of another collective consciousness which had intervened in the extraction of information from the 'Leader' to be considered. There was much here that it did not understand and it felt that what could not be understood must be a threat!

For many millions of years the adult end-product of the Collective had dominated all life-forms it had found. It had travelled from world to world, extending its grip on whatever life-forms it had encountered. The central consciousness had cloned itself many times as the seed-cases had been projected into the cosmos over and over again whenever the Tree felt threatened. It had no way of ever knowing whether its kin had ever made it to another water-world, so it always acted as if it were the only survivor. The Collective had evolved on one of the first planets to bring forth life and had been one of many. A vegetative kind of warfare had taken place as the trees fought for light and air space amongst themselves, until some of them perfected the art of collecting enough fissionable material and exploding the trunk of the Tree beyond orbit, casting the seed-cases into the cosmos to take their chances.

Long ago, the unstable sun that gave birth to the Trees had

exploded, destroying the world of their birth and enriching the stellar wastes with dense materials capable of building more planets. Billions of years later the trees still survived and spread their seeds in the universe that the raptor's Spellbinder had chosen to explore. Each seed was a clone of the previous Tree and carried all its life experiences within it, so still the ruthless competition continued among the survivors of that exploding star. Each clone would seek to dominate any other seed's offspring, if it landed on the world of which it had taken possession. Then a vegetative war would break out using the mobile life-forms as living weapons. They would be genetically altered to become parasitic creatures programmed to seek out the 'Other' and chew away at its roots and branches. Each Tree would develop poisons to counter-act the other's defences. An uneasy stalemate would eventually occur and the Trees would eventually accept that each was equal to the other. When that finally happened, the Trees would cross-pollinate and produce newly genetically-crafted seeds. There would then be a race to collect uranium by the spread of the roots and store it until once again the Trees blasted the seed-cases across the interstellar wastes, leaving some of them behind to start all over again.

Many worlds had been reached and pressed into service throughout this galaxy, but this was the first of the Trees to make contact with intelligent beings. Until this moment, the Collective had lived and exploited by instinct each world that it had dominated. The absorption of the intelligent velociraptors on this world had increased its mental powers of cognisance far ahead of any of its kind. It now had many emotions that lay outside its vegetative mind, including curiosity about everything that it had taken for granted. It was this new window on its existence that held it back from trying to destroy the silent invader. The fleeting contact with the creature's mind had filled its consciousness with a burning desire to know much more about the life-form with which it was sharing this planet.

It waited patiently for the next move by the intruder. As more and more of the velociraptors became its servants, so the capability of its mind increased. As it waited, the survey of this new world continued and its knowledge increased. Now the creatures of the air flew errands for the Collective, building up a concise map of the continent and feeding the results back to the collective mind. There was no hurry to invoke the Quickening for many years yet, as that part of the seeds could remain dormant as long as the Collective deemed necessary. The most important thing was the understanding of the intruder and whether it could use the abilities which interested the Collective. The two things its mind had gleaned from that fleeting contact were that the intruder was from somewhere else. The other was that it could go back again. Could this be a method of spreading its many seeds to other worlds? It would wait and see.

CHAPTER FOUR

The Goblin Spellbinder twisted its way through the multitude of Rifts separating the many different Earths from each other. Chisbolt Hungry-jaw had examined the information stored in the memory banks of his Spellbinder and felt very out of his depth. He worried that his son, who was trapped inside the Raptor's ship, might try something foolish. His family had always been risk takers, which was why they had a goblin ship of their own. They had crewed on the Spellbinders which had rescued the gnomes that had been imprisoned by the dreadful Eloen and had worked with the velociraptors who had spirited them away from under the noses of the Dokka'lfar when Peterkin had struck. He had expected a killing spree that would have wiped out all of Eloen's specially bred Dark Elves. Instead, to the amazement of all the many different breeds of sapient beings, the High King had simply withdrawn from that world after removing the entire stock of human weapons first, leaving them in quarantine.

He had proved to be right. It had taken about five hundred years for all the mental poison of Eloen's mind bending and 'pressing' to leak away. Now the High King's grandchildren no longer hated him; they had slowly understood the derangement of their mother's mind. The human heritage had added something to the mix of elfin genes that ran through their bodies. Somewhere in the latent soup of the human's brain was the ability to move objects with their minds. This was called telekinesis, and it had been witnessed now and again in the humans' history. In an age of darkness - and there were many of those in humankind's history- they had been burnt at the stake for witchcraft.

This was strongest in the grandchildren of Peterkin, the High King, and was Eloen's strange legacy to the new commonwealth of parallel Earths. Once the Elfin geneticists had removed from their DNA the trigger that gave the humans such ridiculously short lifespans, the reasons for their bloody-minded violence all but disappeared. With the successful cloning of the original Spellbinder, it had led to as many of the sentient ships being produced as were needed after the original ten. Now the personalities were different from each other, as many useful minds were assimilated into the gestalt. Only Peterkin's ship carried the minds of the ancient kings and the original programming. The many copies had been trimmed down to what Peterkin had deemed necessary. The one thing the High King had been adamant about was the lack of extensive weaponry carried by each ship. He had allowed each Spellbinder to carry the simple and sturdy weapon that the humans had developed, called an AK-47, and a limited number of clips of ammunition. This was to encourage peaceful solutions to any problems encountered. The other devices were strong light-emitting lasers which would temporarily blind any creature caught in the beam. It was adjustable to between 3.5W & 3,500mW twin diode and could burn through metal as a tight beam or throw a diffused light as a cone which would deter any creature from approaching it.

The years hung heavy on my soul and the death of our first-born son still tugged at my dear wife's heartstrings. She had been the instrument of death that had robbed the world of the evil Eloen. I will never forget the day she slit the Halfling's throat when our son had willingly given his life-force to the tyrant to restore her twisted youth. It lives in my memory still, and did so in my dear Ameela's so sorely that her mind began to fray apart. Elves are not made for acts of violence. Bringing the death of another does not sit as lightly on our souls as it does with humans. I love these people who have given so much to the elves, but at what cost?

My dear mother is ebbing steadily away and nothing that Spencer can do will stay time's arrow. Dawn's early silver light has reached that place where even a long-lived creature like an elf realises that their time has almost finished. The years with Spencer had lifted her soul to great heights, and the two of them had been happy in this stolen time that I had been instrumental in bestowing on them both. I had called him back from the afterlife with the rest of my human friends in a ritual I would not dare to repeat at any cost. As they were all resurrected with my blood, dripped upon their bones, they were reconstituted as Halflings and took on elfin attributes including a much longer lifespan. They also had much stronger telepathic abilities than they had as pure humans when I first altered them.

The years of quarantine had leached out all the mental poisons that had been left behind of Eloen's terrible legacy. My grandchildren had returned to the fold, as I had hoped that they would. I had lost my son, but I had eventually gained the love and trust of the two boys and two girls she had left behind her. Firovel, Cethafin, Brianna and Kellynn had grown into beautiful elves with little of their human attributes, apart from their height and build. My own two sons born after that coupling that Ameela had insisted on, after I had found Eloen's hiding place, were long ago fully grown. One of them would be High King and would have that awful mantle of responsibility to all of our many species. We had called them Petronius and Barathon. They were both silver-haired and had an unsettling way of looking deep into anybody's soul with their bright blue eyes. Both of them were bright and talented elves and both had taken wives that were part Halfling. The children they had produced had the gene that predisposed the telekinetic ability. I knew that soon all of the elfin race would have human genes mixed into their genomes. The dwarves that the humans referred to as Neanderthals lived apart from the humans, enjoying their company, but never getting emotionally involved. There would be no hybrids between these two very different strains of human. The trolls had now acclimatised to a daylight existence and were no longer the secretive race that they had been. All in all I had been satisfied with my stewardship of the parallel worlds, and there had been no objection to my rule.

I had banned all weapons of any complexity as unnecessary and had restricted the armaments aboard the Spellbinders and all across the settled parallel Earths. The bow was sufficient for killing game and as the telepathic powers of the elves could control any of the prehistoric beasts that were used for transporting stonework, force was unnecessary there. The sciences pursued by all the many research stations were directed towards peaceful enterprises. The atomic weapons developed by the humans had been dismantled long ago and the plutonium and uranium dispersed into the sun. All beings lived in harmony and now that Eloen's legacy had been neutralised I had a new people that were being assimilated into the racial mix. Little did I know at that time how much I would need their help in the future!

I was watching the sunset from the balcony of Haven with Ameela when I felt my mother's call. "Peterkin, it's time!"

I squeezed Ameela's hand in mine and she said, "I heard. Let us be there to witness her departure from this plane."

We walked swiftly back into the room that had been prepared for my mother's passing, going under the decorated arch and to the chair that she was sitting in. Henry Spencer was by her side and was kneeling by her side, holding her hand tightly in his coal-black grasp. His other arm was thrown about her shoulders, holding her as close as he could.

"My son," she gasped, "the time allotted on this plane has all but run out for me. I have lived a long life and have no regrets about how I have spent it. You, my beloved son, became High King. Neither of us expected that to happen as it did when you were born. You have been a Great High King, resolute in the responsibility that the mantle of power threw around your shoulders. I am content."

I leaned forward, kissed my mother's forehead and laid my hand across her silver locks of hair. She had dressed in silver and black as befitted a King's mother and her slim body still had the curves of a younger elf underneath the metallic fabric robes. Already her body was losing the self-healing properties that all elves are born with. The crucifixion scars on her hands and feet had appeared and opened up and she was beginning to bleed profusely from them. Once again Eloen's vengeance crossed the years and took its toll. I would never forget the sight of my mother, nailed to a large oak door, when I came to her rescue at the castle, Homecoming, on Alfheimr. Eloen had left my mother, but had taken my son.

Her mind slipped into mine and I felt her love for her only son swell into a crescendo of emotions, along with her love of Spencer, who had been by her side longer than my father had. All at once her body began to fail and both of her heart rates slowed. That quicksilver mind began to retreat from all of us and hide behind the veil of death, and as it did so, I was aware that my dear friend Henry Spencer was singing the Dirge of un-being. As he did so his mind penetrated the veil and joined her on the other side, letting go of his Halfling body.

My dear mother and Spencer were gone. Their bodies slumped together and I reached forward and gently closed their eyes. I was aware that Mellitus was by my side and tears were rolling down his cheeks as he silently stood. I looked around the room and was not surprised to see all my hybrid friends had been here to say their goodbyes to 'Dawn's Early Silver Light' while she was here. Memories there were in all of us of her sitting behind Spencer on a Quetzalcoatlus bearing an AK-47 in her hands, dealing death to the Dokka'lfar. My mother had been an incredible elf and had been the motivating power that had persuaded me to oust the villainous Waldwick from power. When I found out that he had arranged the 'accident' that killed my father, Peter, I had no compunction in using him as the infected bait that helped destroy the Dokka'lfar. I felt the copy of the mind of my father rejoice as she joined him on the other side. He would welcome Spencer as a brother for his care and love for his once wife. Jealousy was an emotion from which elves did not suffer. We believe in free will and with the lifespans that we enjoyed, there was always time to live as we wished.

Since I had resurrected my human friends from the dead, the tomb I had had the dwarves build had remained empty, apart from the Uzbekistanis who had aided me in the struggle to eliminate the Dark Elves once and for all. Eloen soon put paid to that. She had performed the most heinous of acts, the taking of life-force to maintain eternal youth. This is something that any sane elf would not do at any price.

It had been arranged that my mother would be taken to the tomb, but no plans had been made for Spencer. I had been very carefully kept out of range of my friend, Henry, in case I might persuade him not to do what he had done. His remains would be laid with her in the same sepulchre. I had the dwarves cut shallow steps into the mountainside long ago so that my wingless friends could visit this place of solitude quite safely and that a coffin could be taken up and into the tomb without danger. Now there would be two to be taken up. The coffins were light and sparse without any adornments so that when the bodies were laid naked onto their stone shelves, the wooden coffins were discarded. Here they could decompose until only the bones were left as testament to who they once were. This high up the mountainside there were no large carrion eaters to do more than disturb the bones a little and the insects would do the rest. This was why I was able to perform the rite that brought my friends back from the afterlife.

I would miss my mother's shrewd advice and most of all her love for her son. I stood for a while beside my mother and her lover for a few moments longer before signalling the gnomes to take them away. Ameela and I walked back to where we had watched the sunset from the balcony where only the after-glow of the sun still kissed the clouds, turning them red. I felt a little spot of numbness inside my soul where my mother usually dwelt and an emptiness that would never be filled again on this world. I would miss her, but this was the order of things and I knew, as one who had been there, that others would be there to meet her, as one day she would meet me.

It was during the next morning that I received an urgent thought-cast from an old friend as a goblin Spellbinder tore through the Rift above the castle. It was Chisbolt Hungry-jaw, and he was more than a little disturbed.

"High King, activate your Spellbinder and stand by for an information exchange," he spoke in my mind. "The Raptors and their Spellbinder have stumbled into a massive problem.

I am coming directly to see you, as this is so urgent it cannot wait."

After all these years linked together all I needed to do was to think "Spellbinder activate" and my alter ego awoke. It immediately downloaded the information from the goblin ship and transferred the information to me. It was while I was processing the information Chisbolt had channelled to me via the Spellbinder that he burst through the double doors leading to my control room.

"High King! What are we to do? My son is down there on that world doing what he can to help Vinr and the crew of their Spellbinder," the goblin stated.

"He should be safe enough inside the Spellbinder, Chisbolt. How impetuous is your son, old friend? Do you think he will go outside the safety of the vessel?"

"You can bet on it! He will not be content to view the situation from inside! As for Vinr, she is a raptor and you know they all think they are invincible! The information that we brought back from that parallel world shatters any feeling of safety I ever had about the multiverse which is being explored by the use of the elfin ships."

"It would seem that whatever landed on that world has come from another star system. Judging by the speed at which it came in, whatever life-form was in it was able to re-animate after millions of years in the void. Looking at the records from the Raptor's Spellbinder, whatever that thing was it had not been manufactured. I think we are dealing with something that has grown on another world. There seems to be a central seed-case which contained a huge amount of tiny carriers which in turn was loaded with seeds. From what was sent to your ship, all large life-forms seem to be under some kind of mental control. Why and for what purpose we can only guess at until we pay that world a visit."

The goblin heaved a sigh of relief when I said the words "Pay a visit."

I sat back on my throne and turned to the information that Chisbolt's ship had transferred to the original Spellbinder. I watched again the fall through the atmosphere of the seed-case and how it changed shape to suit the conditions with such purpose. The outer husk had soon burnt up, slowing the re-entry speed and releasing the gliding shape beneath it, which had a metal skin. This too had eventually skimmed in and out of the atmosphere, becoming a fireball on final re-entry, and once through that stage had disintegrated into countless large sycamore seed shapes. They dispersed right across the continent and broke open again to show millions of dandelion seed shapes that floated down to earth on a ball of candyfloss. The recording device had caught the moments of contact when the seeds touched living things. They were absorbed into the larger animals and disappeared. What fascinated me was that where they touched one of the raptors indigenous to this planet, they settled onto the back of the head, leaving the stalk protruding and the delicate ball of candy-floss exposed.

The frightening fact was that a life-form from a totally different world had adapted to a different DNA structure and blended with it. This was something the geneticists would need to know about. The human-hybrid, John Smith, was still pottering about in the laboratories beneath the main floors of Haven. Sam Pitts was still living amongst the trolls with No'tt-mjool, with his Night Flower right at the bottom of the castle. The others I had called back from the afterlife were all still here at my castle, joined to others of the elfin races. Mellitus had stayed with me and would not go back amongst his own people, as although they were long-lived, he, being part elf, would see too many of his grandchildren die of old age while he stayed relatively young.

I knew that I had only to ask and these adventurers would come with me with the weak excuse that they were needed to look after me. I knew they were bored with the gentle lives they led and craved a little excitement. I quickly made contact with them all and explained the situation to them. My scientist-engineer was already making a list of what he would need to study this strange life-form. Sam Pitts began a weapons check in the armoury in the lower reaches of the castle. Hoatzin was already selecting the strongest of the Quetzalcoatlus that were penned. Steven and David were saying goodbyes to their wives, packing their own types of supplies which they thought they might need.

Suddenly I became aware of Ameela standing very quiet and still in the main arch that looked out onto the veranda. She walked steadily towards me and stared at me so strangely that a shiver went up my spine.

"I have a bad feeling about this" she said. "I listened in on the information that was passed onto the Spellbinder. We have never had to deal with anything like this. Nothing we have ever had to contend with before is anything like this life form. Think about it! This is an alien life-form that is taking over a complete world. We should leave it alone and call that Rift off-limits to all Spellbinders." She gripped me by the upper arms. "It must never come here! Not one seed can ever come here. Peterkin. I am scared out of my wits. This is nothing like Eloen and her dreams of conquest. This thing is conquest!"

"I cannot leave the raptors and the goblin in that Spellbinder to die" I replied. "Also there are the other velociraptors which are indigenous to that world. Would you leave them in total domination? They use tools, Ameela! They are intelligent beings in their own right and use fire." I was shocked to my core. "I cannot leave those creatures to whatever fate has been wished upon them."

CHAPTER FOUR

"I tell you one thing, Peterkin, I will come with you! You are not leaving me here to wonder what dangers you face. If you must go, take your grandsons with you. Cethafin and Firovel need a purpose in life and some responsibility. Take also our two sons Petronius and Barathon. They too need experience of responsibility as one day they will rule in your stead. That way I can be sure that you will do nothing foolish!"

There was no way I could argue with her, not after so many centuries spent in her company. Her advice had been sound on the many occasions she had given it, and I always listened. What she had declared made sense. That extra sense of telekinesis that my grandchildren possessed might prove more than useful.

Within a week my alter ego, the original Spellbinder, was ready to go. John Smith and his goblin staff had packed it with all kinds of diagnostic equipment and weapons which he had developed over the years against my approval. Meanwhile the copies of the dead Kings' minds constantly worried and agitated about the problem. My father summed it up with the statement that until we had a first-hand view of the situation there was nothing to be gained by speculation. Eventually the rest of them agreed. My mind became quiet and I was able, uneasily, to sleep.

I found it difficult to adjust to a world without my mother in it. I had never realised just how close we had come over the years, ever since I overthrew the mad King Waldwick and took the position of High King of the Ljo'sa'lfar. It was she who had propelled me into taking control after I had rescued Ameela from the Tower of Absolom. Every step of those difficult times she had been by my side, supporting me in her indomitable style. She had sidestepped that position when Ameela had taken her place as consort to me and the title of High Queen settled upon her lovely shoulders. Now she lay quietly rotting with her lover, Spencer, in the family tomb. The other members of the original rescue party were pragmatic about it and accepted the loss of Henry Spencer as something that had been his decision.

We do not grieve over death when it has some purpose, and she had done so much in her life that I did not sorrow to extreme over her timely departure to the afterlife which I knew awaited both of them. I just missed her far more than I ever thought that I would.

Once the news reached me that the Spellbinder was ready to go, I made my way to the control chair that doubled up as my 'throne' and pushed the staff of power into its socket. Everyone had come aboard. The Spellbinder pulled itself from out of the molecular substance of the Haven castle and settled around us like a giant soap bubble. There were plenty of seating arrangements for those who had decided to come and see what news the goblin ship had brought. I was very happy to have that band of adventurous mercenaries at my side again. With Sam Pitts came the troll maiden, No'tt-mjool, her abilities honed and sharpened by the passing years. Her mother, Sees-far (Vita-fjarri) was also 'Spakr-Kona' or wise woman to the trolls. She had been their Queen for many centuries and had been the one I went to for advice during the time of Eloen's revenge. Night Flower had been with Sam Pitts ever since that time, and because the genetic drift was too great, they were childless. Now those times were past, as both of them were beginning to show the passing years as well as I. My blond hair had long ago become shot with silver, as had the lemon colour of Ameela's locks. She and I wore it long about our shoulders in a plait bound with golden wire.

I called Sam and Night Flower to my presence before we set off and let the Spellbinder float off the edge of my veranda.

"What can you see ahead? Is there anything that I need to know before we set out across the Rifts?" I asked.

"I can see us arriving in orbit about a world similar to this one," the troll maiden replied. There is no danger there that I can sense, but there are so many multiplicities to be had that I cannot say beyond that point in time."

I exerted the power of my mind to the goblin ship and said, "We are going now, Chisbolt. Follow me and do nothing rash when we get there!"

With that the Spellbinder opened the Rift above the castle and we started to skip through the many realities to that universe where the raptors had mistakenly landed their Spellbinder.

CHAPTER FIVE

We followed the trace through the Rifts that the goblin Spellbinder had used, as it was the quickest way to find the alternative Earth that the Raptors had discovered. Chisbolt gave me a warning that we were fast approaching the world they had been surveying when the Raptors had slid past them. As we passed through the warp in reality, beneath us shone an icy world almost entirely covered in glaciers, with two enormous polar caps that extended a third of the way across the planet. Ice a mile deep covered the lands and reached over the seas, anchoring them into the continents. There was little trace of Europe or Canada, as the ice extended beyond the borders of Texas and into Mexico. As for the southern regions, they too had been buried under the glaciers, leaving the sea bottoms exposed until the continental shelf dropped away. I could see what the attraction would be to the cold-loving goblins on this alternative Earth. The southern shores of the Mediterranean coastline and what had been desert over Africa were covered in forests and veldt, mile after mile all around the globe. It could stay that way for millions of years until things warmed up again and the great melt began.

I projected my thoughts to the goblin ship and said, "A good world for goblin-kind to live upon. You have found a treasure you are welcome to exploit. We will miss your people, Chisbolt Hungry-jaw!"

I got a quick reply. "High King! We may move some of my people here, but not all. We live within the Elfin Commonwealth and are proud to be part of it. Vinr was not exploring to leave Haven, she was just being independent. The raptors are progressing well in their own ruthless way. Any one of us could have made contact with this creature and followed it down to the surface without realising the danger."

I agreed with him and concentrated with the Spellbinder on what Rift to open and close to arrive at the Raptors' dinosaur world. We passed an Earth in which the moon was spiralling closer and would eventually collide. It raised huge tides that drowned the lands twice a day and washed away all chance of life except on much higher grounds and mountain valleys. Excessive volcanic activity added to the unpleasantness of this tortured planet.

At last we approached the Rift that contained the dinosaur world and a feeling of deep apprehension shivered up my spine. I looked towards Ameela, only to see her stare at me wide-eyed as we slipped through.

No'tt-mjool stumbled to her knees, gave a shuddering gasp and held her hands to her black curly-haired head. Sam Pitts held her tightly and gave her support as she rocked to and fro. This all happened as the two Spellbinders skipped out of the last Rift and took synchronous orbit above the grounded ship far below. I could feel the power of the mind that had taken charge of all the larger living creatures on that planet. It was awesome in its reach. We would need to wear the iron collars to block out this dominating being if we went down there.

I tunnelled through and projected my mind far below to make contact with Vinr and Nuzac immediately. "Are you unharmed?" I asked. "What is the situation down there?"

Nuzac replied, "So far no real damage, apart from the fact

that we have this thing's seeds embedded in the walls of the Spellbinder and we can't get them out. Otherwise we would have pulled out of here long ago. Also we are back on ship's rations as we ate the dino we killed some time ago. We were beginning to worry that we would need to go out there again to snaffle another one before we started to starve!"

"My goblin friend exaggerates, High King. We have plenty of rations and fresh water to rehydrate them, but the diet is monotonous for meat-eaters like ourselves," Vinr stated. "I also have young to feed and they follow Nuzac around, waiting for him to fall over or show any signs of weakness."

"Can you not feel the power of that mind?"

"We have felt it all the time we have been here. We wear the iron torcs most of the time to help keep it out. It wants us to become part of the Collective, whatever that means. Can you get us out of here?"

"Give me time. We have only just got here. Be assured that we will do all that we can to get you out," I replied, and glanced across at the troll maiden, who was still holding her head in Sam's lap as she had now collapsed onto the floor. "We have some problems of our own at the moment that need addressing."

I felt the mind of the raptor Vinr reach out to mine and ask, "What about the people that have been taken by the Collective? We cannot depart from here and leave them as its puppets!"

That thought was uppermost in my mind also. Although these simpler versions of the velociraptors were not part of the Elfin Commonwealth, they were sentient beings; tool and fire users. That made them part of my responsibilities, or I would judge myself as Dokka'lfar in my heart, and that was something I would not do.

My sons and grandchildren gathered round the command

chair and generated a shield effect around me as I probed the collective mind far down beneath us. They formed a chain down to the Spellbinder, ready to pull my mind out as quick as thought itself. The two granddaughters, Brianna and Kellynn, formed an anchor with Ameela, feeding out a funnel surrounding my identity. My sons, Petronius and Barathon, made two points of the square with my grandsons, Firovel and Cethafin, at the other points. Centred in this protected position hung my consciousness, probing the outermost edges of the being we had come to know as the Collective.

I made contact with a velociraptor that had been left to watch Vinr's Spellbinder while the others were being directed to other tasks. To my horror I realised that the poor creature was starving and had not been instructed to eat. I gently eased into her mind and did my best to circumvent the rigid conditioning that had been inserted by this alien usurper. She had been standing motionless for several days without sleep or rest and immediately fell into a twitching heap. The agonising pain of cramped muscles sent her into oblivion before she could scream.

I quickly directed Vinr and Nuzac to exit the Spellbinder wearing the impenetrable suits made of elf-stone and attend to her needs with water and food. Once I was sure that help was on its way, I returned my mind into the thread that connected back into the mind of the Collective. The source of the connection was a seed that was rooted into the spinal column and from there into the raptor's brain. This made a telepathic link to all the other seeds that were rooted into every creature that had become a host. The mind of the Collective lived in all of these multitudes of different species, and it was incredibly old. I felt it waken to my presence and gain strength as it drew on the combined minds of the hosts that it inhabited.

I disconnected from the link and left it frantically searching for the invading mind. I rapidly slipped into many different hosts, working my way along the shores of the swamp and drawing the Collective mind away from the grounded Spellbinder. No matter what the entity tried it could not find me, and I became aware as the moments passed by that this thing had not experienced a situation like this. It had no intelligence of its own and had only attained this state of consciousness because of the velociraptors which had become unwilling hosts for its seeds.

This was a creature that up until now had relied on instinct to survive, and a very basic kind of intelligence. Absorbing all of the minds of the velociraptors into its collective consciousness had given it self-awareness for the very first time. Its brush with Vinr and a goblin mind had shaken it to its core. It was now aware of further horizons, and was greedily interested in achieving a greater awareness. As my mind swept over the continent I was painfully aware of the scope of this organism and the millions of creatures held in its thrall. Try as I might I could not get to grips with what was referred to as 'the Quickening' and quantify it. I had extracted a great deal of information from the momentary contacts with the minds of each host I had touched, leaving nothing of mine behind me.

The amount of organization that the entity had imposed upon the multitudes of different types of dinosaurs was awesome. It became mentally stronger by absorbing every velociraptor's mind and casting out the almost mindless creatures that it had inhabited at the first initial contact. Before it did this, however, it took the animals to a central place to die. This place was to be the focal point of the raptor's new purpose in life.

Having seen enough, I returned my consciousness back to Vinr and Nuzac and the starving raptor. Nuzac had blocked the telepathic control that the organism had imposed over the raptor, while Vinr fed her and also made sure that she drank sparingly. Both of them made sure that they did not touch the feathery growth that projected from the back of her neck. There was a bulge as big as my fist anchored underneath the flesh and it appeared to have become part of her. A stalk projected from this lump and stood proudly upwards, with a fine forest of tiny feathery spokes looking like a ball of fluff spreading from the tip.

Separated from the influence of the Collective, the female raptor was now aware of this thing growing inside her and was terrified as the telepathic antennae caught her eye. She reached up to grasp the stalk to pull it out and screamed in terror, as the thing would not remove itself from the back of her neck. In her frenzied haste she made the stalk bleed and stripped some of the feathery growth from the end. Vinr held onto her upper arms tightly to stop her from ripping the growth out and made her sit down upon a nearby rock.

I took over the blocking effect from the goblin and ordered them back inside the Spellbinder, where they would be separated from the growth behind the raptor's head. I summoned Firovel to my mental side and directed him to send his mind inside the raptor and trace the invasive growth.

"Can you remove it?" I asked.

"Not unless we bring her on board and I spend many hours tracing each nerve and root! Whatever that thing is, it is part of her nervous system. It's as if she has another brain wired into the one she was born with. The more I study it the more I am sure I could not remove it without killing her, Grandfather."

"Stop her heart" I replied, sending her into unconsciousness. "I must return to the Spellbinder along with all of you maintaining the shield. She will die slowly of hunger and thirst as the thing controlling her has left her here to watch without instructing her to feed. It would be kinder to let her die swiftly than just leave her here."

Firovel did as I instructed and pinched her arteries shut by telekinesis, starving the heart. She quickly died. We retracted back inside the Spellbinder, leaving the other ship still grounded. I quickly shared the knowledge I had taken from the many hosts I had skimmed through. We now knew that an organism that referred to itself as the Collective was organising the animals and the intelligent velociraptors for some future purpose that we were not sure about. Given that the growth behind the raptor's head had become part and parcel of the host it had taken over, there seemed little that we could do at the moment. The one thing I had been all too aware of was the immense mind that was scattered across the continent below us. Ridding the grounded Spellbinder of the 'seeds' that had burrowed into the fabric of the ship was still a difficult task. We could not dare risk bringing one of those seeds back with us to Haven. For all we knew, the thing could multiply, taking over host after host.

The Spellbinders were sentient beings in their own right and tossing the ship into the sun was a last resort. Leaving it down there was also foolish, just in case the Collective could gain control over it and use it to spread its seeds through the multiverse.

I looked across at Ameela and remembered her words. She had said, "I have a bad feeling about this. I listened in on the information that was passed onto the Spellbinder. We have never had to deal with anything like this. Nothing we have ever had to deal with before is anything like this life form. Think about it. This is an alien life-form that is taking over a complete world. We should leave it alone and call that Rift off-limits to all Spellbinders. It must never come here." By 'here'

I knew that she meant Haven and all the other parallel worlds we were developing.

As I came back to my body I said to Ameela, "There has to be an answer. I cannot leave them down there to die. We are not fools. Elves are creatures that can always find a way out of a problem."

"What did we do about the Dokka'lfar, Peterkin? We ran away until you made a stand. It always seems to come down to you, High King. I am afraid, dearest love! I am so afraid," she sobbed and turned away from the control chair, running from the room.

I did not know what to say to her retreating back and slumped into the chair to think. Firovel shared his examination of the raptor's nervous system with his siblings to show how the seed had implanted itself into the spinal column and the dinosaur's brain. I too examined all the information he had brought back and could see no alternative to what I had ordered him to do. I closed them out of the mental loop and asked the advice of the long-dead kings. Again, just as Ameela had said, we had never had to deal with anything like this in all our struggles in the past. I felt that first we had to remove the embedded seeds from the grounded Spellbinder.

I spoke to Deedlit's copied mind about the possibility of taking the ship into orbit and falling back to earth as a fireball, thus cooking the seeds where they lay. He sadly reminded me that the spellbinders warped reality to move from Rift to Rift and also to manoeuvre. The ship was not designed for re-entry at those temperatures. The nannite construction that allowed the vessel to assume any shape it needed would come apart with the burning heat.

Whilst I was contemplating the alternatives, John Smith interrupted my thoughts with a possible solution.

"Get them to take the Spellbinder into orbit, transfer the

crew to our ship. Ruthlessly slice that part of the ship that is infected away from the rest of the main body and send it on its way towards the sun. Once all the air has been loosed into space, instruct the artificial intelligences to reconstruct with what is left. That way we will make sure the ship is clean of any infection. The crew can then return to the ship and we can consider what we are going to do about the situation on the planet below. The thing that bothers me is what sort of information transfer we are doing by being host to those seeds."

That was something that had not occurred to me, and I began to wonder. I asked, "What are you worried about, John?"

His thought came straight back to me and chilled my soul. "The manipulation of the Rifts, High King. If the intelligence learns how to deploy the gateways, it can spread its seeds throughout the multiverse. We have to kill it!"

"I cannot do that without destroying every velociraptor on the planet below. We must learn more about this creature before we do anything. I cannot snuff out a potential partner in the commonwealth that we have built together," I protested. "That would be the Dokka'lfar way of dealing with the problem. I am Ljo'sa'lfar and I will not sentence these creatures to oblivion. There has to be another way. Contact Vinr and tell her to do as you have explained, while I give this matter more thought."

Meanwhile the Collective had reacted to the death of one of its many servants by shifting the view to one of the giant beasts feeding quietly near the grounded ship. The range of its intellect was expanding as more and more of the velociraptors came under its range of influence. The new thoughts filled its expanding mind and led to so many different avenues that it had seemed almost mindless in its earlier states of existence on the previous worlds. It had glimpsed a much more complicated world through the mind of the raptor, regarding what it now knew as a goblin. In that fleeting glimpse it had also learnt about other creatures known as Elves. This was the mind that it had chased over the continent without any success in capturing its thoughts. The strength of this mind overshadowed the puny intellects of the tool-using life forms under its thrall. It had been so well protected that it had slipped through every mental noose it had thrown over the hosts that it had briefly dominated. It was also aware that the mind of the Collective had been infiltrated and information had leaked out.

A completely new emotion filled its mind - anger. Instinctively the Collective knew that it must master these aberrations or suffer the consequences. It was aware of the vast oceans of time that lay behind it and its instincts to hasten the 'Quickening' were difficult to rein in, as it realised that more information needed to be taken from these creatures that had come from another world. Where they had come from was an unknown territory about which it needed to know much more. How they had arrived in orbit around this world presented vast possibilities for the newly-burgeoning intellect to explore for itself.

In the middle of the Collective's thoughts it suddenly became aware that the first object filled with free minds had detached itself from the ground and was floating upwards. The seeds embedded in the fabric passed on as yet unintelligible information about how this was done. The Collective stored the knowledge for future examination, but for the moment it followed its seeds ever upwards - until something happened that it could not understand. A bright light sliced the object apart, casting the implanted seeds and part of the object towards the sun. it now began to lose all contact with the seeds, as the intense cold of space froze them solid and put them into hibernation.

Once the Raptor's Spellbinder achieved orbit, it spun round to make sure that the seeds could not transfer to Peterkin's ship and the crew disembarked. They left the sentient ship to exhaust all traces of air and to rearrange its contours to place the seeds that had penetrated the fabric of the ship in isolation. This operation could never have been tried on the surface of the alternative Earth, as they had penetrated far too close to where the sentient minds of the Spellbinder were stored. First the ship had to solidify and transfer the memory banks away to a safer place away from the embedded seeds. It then grew an umbrella in front of the part carrying the seeds, to stop the sun's rays from warming them up. John had surmised that the intense cold would send the seeds back safely into hibernation. By the time the package reached the sun it would not be a problem, as the star devoured it.

The Raptor's Spellbinder detached itself from my ship and rotated around to give my friend, John, a clear view of the infected part. The ship had changed shape and had extended the seed-embedded section so that the heavy-duty laser could do its work. John Smith collected the sun's energy into the receptors and redirected them to focus onto the elf-stone still attached to the other Spellbinder and vaporise the link. Once the infected part had drifted far enough away, Vinr's ship spun on its axis and slapped the infected part towards the sun with an extended arm. The ship then made contact with my vessel and filled itself with air and warmth.

I called a meeting with Vinr, Nuzac, my grandchildren, my sons and my scientifically-minded elf-human friend, John Smith. I also included all of my elf-human compatriots, along with the Troll Night Flower.

All minds were open, and I started with the biggest problem - the ethics involved.

"This is what we know," I started. "We have on the planet's

surface a dilemma. This invading life form is now intelligent, and while it has taken hold of the velociraptors that are indigenous to this world, it has not harmed them intentionally. The lower orders of life it is using in a different way. These it regards as expendable and it is driving them to a central point, herded by the raptors. As my grandson has found out, we cannot separate the attached seeds from their hosts without killing them. Its mind is scattered all over the continent below us, so there is no central nervous system to attack. There is a hidden agenda that has leaked out to my probing mind, and that is something it calls 'The Quickening'. What that means I just cannot say as yet. Has anyone any ideas or points that we should consider?"

My grandson, Cethafin, spoke up and said, "The solution seems obvious to me. Carpet bomb this whole continent with the device you exploded above mother and the rest of us, until all traces of the Collective are eradicated. You have to be ruthless about the situation. If this life form can learn how to manipulate the Rifts and spread its seeds throughout the multiverse, we will all feel the edge of its domination."

"Cethafin, I cannot destroy the creatures that are hooked into the Collective with an EMP exploded over their heads. They would more than likely die and a whole potential intelligent species would be lost. There has to be another way. We still do not know enough about this organism and what its next stage is. All we have seen are the seeds of the mature organism. We have no idea what comes next." I stared at my grandson in disbelief.

"Grandfather, please listen to me. That is a possible solution and you have to consider it as a last resort. Yes, I completely realise that it is a Dokka'lfar solution to this problem and that makes it unacceptable to you. Nevertheless it has to be considered, as the risks are too high. Whatever we do here, this intelligence that has a whole continent in thrall must never leave here. I fully understand the horror you feel about possibly snuffing out an intelligent species, but I insist that it is considered."

The mind of Vinr entered the debate with a flat statement. "If the worst comes and we have no choice, then these people will have to be put to death along with this Collective intelligence. They are a primitive race, but they exist on other parts of this world, so taking the long view that I am used to with elfin lines of thought, we should kill them."

"If we miss one seed, this could happen again in the future," I answered. "We cannot be sure that some of the seeds were blown over the seas and over the other reaches of this world. I have taken the suggestion to heart, my friends, but I must insist that we study this organism more closely before I decide what to do. John Smith, I want you to go back to Haven and from there find whatever devices we might need to put this world to death. Meanwhile, while you are gone on Chisbolt's Spellbinder I must look for another way to tackle this problem."

I broke up the meeting and stared at the beautiful planet that spun lazily below us, desperately racking my brains for an alternative solution.

CHAPTER SIX

John Smith had transferred to the goblin Spellbinder with Chisbolt and was making his way back to Haven, and from there he would be looking for the Hell weapons that had been developed on Earth centuries before. Peterkin had long ago instructed John to make sure that all of these devices were deactivated. The plutonium necessary to arm them had been separated into small parcels and deposited far underground well away from each other to decay radioactively. It would still take hundreds of thousands of years before the material became inert.

John could remember as if it were yesterday leading a team of goblins along with the few atomic physicists who had survived the terrorists' 'flash war' that had decimated his home planet. Using a modified Spellbinder they had tunnelled through solid granite by placing the vessel out of phase with the rest of the universe and had sunk through like a hot knife in butter. Peterkin had him place the weapons out of reach of any being, without access to one of the sentient ships. The centuries that had passed had not dulled his memory at all and the human-elf hybrid that he had become, due to Peterkin's calling his soul back from the afterlife, still remained youthful.

The team had built a tomb far below ground, with extended tunnels for miles like the spokes of a wheel. At the end of each tunnel was a lead-lined box which contained plutonium at less than critical level. Now he would have to assemble a team together again from the goblins who were still alive and had been part of the decommissioning. The humans who had been with him were long gone, but his descendants had followed the scientific path and would agree to help.

Fortunately Chisbolt Hungry-jaw knew many of the families which had members of the original team and knew where to find them. John knew that the task with which Peterkin had entrusted him was possible, but how long it would take was impossible to know. The level of technology of the Elfin Commonwealth was not at an advanced level, as Peterkin had kept it that way. Medical science had blossomed along with the melding of elfin knowledge and physics, but weapons were kept at a simple level. Projectile weapons had never been advanced beyond the AK-47s that had been used in the Elf war, as there was no need for them. The Spellbinders were all lightly armed as a matter of policy, to prevent any chance of conflict occurring if a more advanced race of beings were ever met. A peaceful way would be found for any dispute that might transpire and failing that, the Rift would be marked as 'Do not open' and left in quarantine.

Unfortunately this was not possible with this alternative Earth which was dominated by the Collective, because if the creature mastered the manipulation of the Rifts, it could spread throughout the multiverse. John Smith shuddered when he thought about that possibility and grimly determined that if necessary he would bring back enough hydrogen bombs to turn that world into a radioactive wasteland, if there were no alternative. It sickened him just to think about it, and the fact that there were intelligent, tool-using velociraptors there made it worse. He was heartily relieved that it was not his responsibility. He had done the High King's bidding now for over five hundred years and had found him exceptionally fair and wise in all his decisions. He had never regretted being resurrected and had enjoyed the second long life that Peterkin had bestowed on him. This had facilitated his pursuit of elvish science with both elves and goblins to take him into strange areas of physics. There were so many advantages of being part elf, besides the much longer life and not losing your memory over the long years. Also, he never became ill and any injuries would heal within a very short time.

He well remembered when they had taken down Peterkin's mother from being crucified on the oak door. The marks of the nails had sealed and healed as he watched. He had aged over the centuries and now his hair was silver, but his body had stood the test of time and remained looking middle-aged. Now human beings lived to his age as a matter of course, and this had affected the once-violent behaviour of his species. The very idea of violence was now abhorrent to all humans and none felt the need to carry weapons. He regretted the destruction of the Earth and the laying waste of so much of his home world, but he accepted that the end result justified the new elfin regime. Humanity now lived side by side on the elfin worlds with many of the eldritch species of folklore, and all benefited by the interaction.

The awesome weapons that he had been sent to find and put into working order filled him with disgust and horror. He had seen with his own eyes what awful destruction they could do on his home planet. Now Peterkin might have to unleash these weapons of mass destruction onto a defenceless world to halt the spread of a life form which was stranger than anything he had ever confronted. Once again he felt happier that it would not be his decision, and his regard for his elfin friend grew even stronger.

"You are very quiet, John Smith," Chisbolt said, breaking in on his thoughts.

"I have much on my mind, Chis, old friend. What Peterkin has asked me to do is beyond your understanding. These weapons that he has asked me to re-locate and put in working order have destructive capabilities far beyond your imagination. I am talking of hundreds of square miles vaporised and thousands of square miles burnt to ash. On top of that will be radioactive fallout that will kill all life wherever it falls."

"It is a last resort. The High King will seek other ways to defeat this problem if he can. Peterkin will have that decision to make if all else fails. Be assured he will not lightly unleash these weapons upon a defenceless world."

"Knowing that makes my task no easier, Chis. I have seen what these weapons can do. Much of my home world is dead and will remain so for hundreds of thousands of years. I still mourn for my childhood world that is gone for ever."

John took the goblin's spindly hands in his. "Will you assist me in this task using your Spellbinder to carry out the mission? It will take a steady hand to coerce the Spellbinder minds to do this. I have the co-ordinates locked in my mind and it will entail taking this ship between the spaces that exist inside the very atoms beneath Haven castle."

The greenish colour drained from Chisbolt's face and he went very pale.

"Who else would be adventurous enough but a goblin captain like me! Scares the shit out of me, but I would have not have forgiven you if you had asked for someone else. I can only worry and wonder what Nuzac will be getting up to with the High King as he tries to think of another solution to the problem."

* * *

I had reached the conclusion that nothing could be gained by staying in orbit, and I put my idea to the others of my extended family.

"We need to go down there and study first-hand what exactly is going on between the creatures controlled by the Collective. What we cannot do is to risk the Spellbinder by taking it down there. Those of you that are coming with me will have to drop from about two miles up and parachute down there, so that the controlling life form will not notice that we have surreptitiously infiltrated its domain. I need the telekinetic abilities of my grandchildren and Vinr to act as a bridge to the indigenous raptors. More eyes and ears would be welcome and Night Flower's precognitive abilities would certainly come in handy.

"Once we are down, pressing the help of some of the untouched dinosaurs into service should give those who are wingless more mobility and also provide protection to the group. This Spellbinder will be able to manufacture suits for all of us to wear and will control our descent. We will go lightly armed, as I do not want any of these captive people to lose what life they have because of our mistakes. They cannot help what they have become and I want all of you to remember that above all else." I stopped and waited for them to make up their minds.

Hoatzin interrupted with his typically pragmatic attitude and said, "We did not come all this way just to sit and watch. You go down there, High King and we all go. It's about time we got some excitement after all these years."

Sam nodded and added, "Night Flower says that all projected futures show that we all go down together, leaving the Spellbinder in orbit above us. Beyond that point she cannot tell you until we are all down. She advises however that your two sons, Petronius and Barathon, remain here to apply any backup that is required. With those two here she feels that the possible outcome will be more successful."

Ameela stood, faced me and flatly stated, "I will not let you go down there without me. Do not even think it, Peterkin! Whatever we have to face down there, we will face it together. Live or die, I will not be separated from you."

I looked across to the troll, who nodded once to confirm what Ameela had said. I felt a fleeting twinge of sorrow from No'tt-mjool as she did this, but I knew that whatever the outcome would be, in that future Ameela had to be included. The long-dead kings reminded me of duty and the responsibility of being High King. I concentrated my will and shut them out, except for one, my father, Peter.

He responded with these words, "My son, heavy is the load that you have to bear. A load that never came to me, I must admit. Yet in all your many dealings and conclusions, you have been fair. Whatever you have to do on this world, I am sure you will do the right thing. This is your nature and you were born to be High King, far more than I ever was." Then my father faded away to that part of my mind he rested in.

Whilst my mind had interrogated the infected Raptor, I had become aware that the others of her kind were acting as shepherds to the large dinosaurs and guiding them to a central position on the Great Plains beneath us. I had the nagging feeling that this was where we needed to go to gain more information about this organism. The continent that was host to the Collective was what would have become Europe and Asia, and its central point was where Lipetsk in Russia would have been. Here the countryside was flat and well watered. Why this was important to the invading intelligence we had yet to discover.

*　　*　　*

For the first time in the long lifespan of the Collective, the composite mind was considering a plan of action which was very different from any it had followed before. In all its past incarnations it had been a totally solitary growth which had chosen to dominate the world it had seeded from one position. There had been competition from time to time against others of its kind and a compromise exacted. Now coherent thoughts on a scale that had never happened before chased different scenarios and alternative possibilities. Before it had acted on instinct alone and that had stood it in good stead, but now it had attained sapience. As the mind grew into more complexity it began to understand that what could very well be a competitive life form had also arrived on this world from somewhere else. So far it had done the Collective no harm, but that could change.

The fleeting glimpses it had stolen from the contact with the creature it now knew as a goblin and the other Raptor had shown it that there were many more worlds for the taking. It had also chased after a very complicated mind without making contact. This mind had shown that it was on a far superior level to itself. If only it could absorb this creature's consciousness, it would then be able to operate on a much higher level.

It recognised the species through the goblin mind as an elf. No matter what it tried, the mind had proved elusive, but it left traces. The Collective studied those glimpses into this other consciousness and could not as yet feel any threat. These were new thoughts that slipped in and out of its awareness.

The seeds that had rooted in the fabric of the entity, which was full of independent minds, had sent back some strange signals when the object had risen through the air. All the time its seeds had orbited this world, it had managed to look through its senses back down at where its central intelligence had chosen to take root. It was amazed at the true size of the world below, and this had set a train of thought through its consciousness. Its seeds had drifted all around this world, and there was a huge area of landmass that would benefit from its organising abilities. The intelligent hosts were everywhere on this world and spread over the lands wherever the large creatures foraged for vegetarian food. As it added more and more of them to the Collective mind it grew in sapience, and true to its unique species, it absorbed the understanding of the way this world's eco-system worked.

A new thought began to expand in the Collective's mind; the idea of communication through language. It had never needed to communicate with any life form before in any of its previous incarnations. Through this method of communication, greater understanding began to grow.

By now there were very few places where the seeds had not penetrated and rooted into animals it could find useful. It broadened its scope and sent the Quickening signal to all of its seeds, concentrating its mind on settling in as many locations as were suitable. Now there would be hundreds of its kind rooting deeply into the fertile soil with one mind, spread all over this world and controlling every living thing worth using.

* * *

I gathered together the members of the reconnoitre party and we all took on an impenetrable skin of elf-stone which John Smith called nannite. On the off-chance that seed-fall was not completely over, I wanted to be sure that we would not be infected by a chance encounter. With our wings tucked up underneath the protective covering we would all be at the mercy of the parachutes which the Spellbinder had prepared and designed into our suits. Once we were far enough down to feel enough air pressure, the backs of our suits would split open and our wings could then be applied. The others among us that were wingless would have to make it all the way down by parachute. Sam Pitts and his men had all done what they referred to as 'drops', but never from two miles high.

No'tt-mjool had never ever tried this at all and was keeping her terror tightly reined in. I assured her that the Spellbinder would be overseeing control all the way down. All she had to do was hang ready in the dual harness and flex her knees on impact when landing. Sam would take her down. The air would be breathable at this height, but bitter cold, so holding our breath because of the cold would do, but all of us would be wearing enclosed helmets for the jump.

My son Barathon eased the Spellbinder out of orbit and slipped through the local Rifts until the ship hovered about two miles high. We were over a hundred miles from the centre of the alien creature's shepherding point. Petronius came with us to make sure that we all dropped safely through the opening onto the world below. We all carried survival packs and the others carried an AK-47 with plenty of clips of ammunition. I fully intended that this would be a last resort and we would use our mental capabilities to ensure our survival. Any life form down there not connected to the Collective would be easily coerced into doing our bidding. Sam, Hoatzin, David and Steven all carried C4, plastic explosives and the necessary fuses in case we needed them. We all had a map of the area beneath us imprinted in our minds and there was a central hill with a good view of the terrain that we all would be heading for. Mellitus carried the one M16 rifle that I had allowed to be broken out of storage, tested and broken down to a kit. He was also carrying a great number of clips of ammunition which he insisted he could carry.

The Halflings all went first, as they would control the paragliding chutes, and we soon dropped through the floor to follow them. I carried Vinr in the same way that Sam carried Night Flower, in front of me. It was not long before we could feel the air bite into the chutes as they inflated and took the load. My young Raptor passenger held onto her sheer terror at falling a mile through the air and trusted her life to me. We could see quite clearly the paragliding humans and Mellitus far below us.

As we all felt the change in the air about halfway down, our suits reclaimed the cords and material and the backs split open, freeing our wings. Now we felt in control, and we powered down in a long glide towards the hill that stood out from the jungle of trees and scrubland below us. The extra weight of Vinr meant that all I could do was to glide towards the landing point.

One by one the paragliding teams dropped onto the hill, and they had already established a parameter of defensive capability by the time we got there.

As we came down, my eyes were drawn to the nesting site of a flock of Quetzalcoatlus that had taken over the cliffside. The Spellbinder had seen them on long-range senses. Our landing had been noticed, and a chorus of hisses greeted our arrival. Those that were in the air had panicked and pulled away from the brightly-coloured chutes, leaving the top of the hill bare.

I attempted a slight upward lift to kill my speed and succeeded. As we landed, I folded my wings and tucked them out of the way, released Vinr, walked over to the group and said, "Our mounts await us, my friends. Each one of you must press the tiny minds of these flying creatures into our service. I could not feel the presence of the Collective in this congregation of dragons, so pick out the strongest and make sure that the rest of them view us as not food. Come grandchildren, now is the time to show me what skills you have and what mind control you are capable of."

Ameela put her hand on mine and said, "They have come a long way from those dark days when we exiled them after I killed their mother. A few centuries of living off the land without any help of technology and only their wits to help them finally made a difference to their attitude towards us. You were right at the time not to have them stripped of their powers and left to die. Even then you could see the potential they represented, once the evil of Eloen had been sponged from their minds. Always you have been the High King in all your dealings with any and every problem you have encountered. I just hope that you will be proved right again, because one day things may go against you."

"If and when they do, my queen, I hope that you will still have advice for me that will give me the inspiration to turn things around" I replied. "I have always listened to you and heeded your guidance. You are at my side this very moment. I could not wish for more." I gave her hand a gentle squeeze. "Now let us pick out a sturdy mount for the long journey ahead."

As we made our way towards the nesting site we could almost taste the smell of these carrion eaters on our tongues. This rookery had to be centuries old, and by the amount of droppings stuck to the rocks, there had been maybe thousands of years of colonisation. Our mounts at the castle had become used to being washed and kept as clean as possible, but these wild creatures were not so fussy. By the expressions on my granddaughters' faces they were not at all keen on mounting these giant flying creatures.

"Grandfather," Brianna exclaimed, "have you seen the state of these dragons? They are covered in filth! How can we ride them in this state?"

"May I suggest that you use your unique mental gifts and remove the mess with your minds? Must I think for you? While you are about it perhaps you could clean all the mounts so that the smell does not warn all the creatures on the plains that we are coming," I suggested, and smiled at her changing expression.

Kellynn, Cethafin and Firovel joined in and soon the Quetzalcoatlus mounts were in a more respectable state as the telekinetic abilities of my grandchildren came into play. Bridles had been brought with us and enough elf-stone had been multiplied by the Spellbinder now in orbit to provide us with comfortable saddles. John Smith had tried several times to explain nanotechnology to me. I never understood it, but I did know how to use it to my advantage. As I once told him, "I do not need to make a gun to fire one."

My grandchildren had made an excellent job of cleaning the flying creatures and not a speck of excrement had been left stuck to their leathery hides. None of the 'dragons' had been touched by the 'seeds', so we did not have a set of spying eyes along with us. To the Collective's senses, we would only register as a flight of Quetzalcoatlus, as long as we kept our thoughts to ourselves by using the iron collars loosely fastened about our necks. We had to strike a medium between shutting out the questing thoughts of the invader and controlling our flying mounts. As their minds were small and we were almost sitting on their heads, this was not difficult.

Communication between ourselves was kept to a minimum. Vinr's mount I managed to tune to the raptor's thoughts so that it would obey her needs. Fortunately she had ridden a dragon several times before at Castle Haven, though never a wild one.

We launched from the rookery towards the central point the dinosaurs were all heading to, unaware that this was happening all over this world. Below us were the plains which on the Earth world would have been the beginning of the Russian Steppes. Vast areas of forest, lakes, rivers and open plains stretched for mile after mile. In the open areas groups of dinosaurs were slowly plodding their way towards some far central point, guided by what I was sure were velociraptors. I got the attention of the others and pointed downwards, making a spiral motion, and watched as my friends altered course and eased the 'dragons' down towards the plains.

My family followed them down towards a convenient hill that rose from the flat plains. A river flowed around the base of its cliffs and I could see that a large group of sauropods were making their way across, mounted by raptors. This was something that would have never happened in nature without mental control. Only the servants of the Collective would be able to do this.

I needed to know more about this creature, and to do so I would need to speak through a 'host' and make contact with it surreptitiously without being recognised as a threat. This was what I needed my grandchildren for on this mission, and I had thought it through very carefully before we had left the Spellbinder behind.

After pressing our mounts to stay put, I led my gifted ones to the edge of the cliff that dropped down to the river and said, "What I want you to do is to pluck one of those raptors from its seat, unconscious, so that the Collective will not notice that it has gone and the others do not notice. How close do you have to be?"

Cethafin answered, "We need to combine our minds and reach out as close as we can get to one of them. If we wait and hide at the base of the cliffs where they enter the water, I think we can pick one off without being seen. Leave it to us."

The four grandchildren climbed back onto their mounts and took to the air, guiding the wild Quetzalcoatlus down towards the river. I watched as these amazing children of my nemesis, Eloen, applied their incredible talents. They had been born in blood and 'mind-pressed' by their mother to hate me and all that I stood for. Their elfin heritage had won over their minds in the end and my son's death had not been in vain.

I still missed Elthred and still relived the moment that he had given his life to the Halfling to give her back her youth. That moment had lasted for a few brief seconds, as Ameela had cut her throat in front of her children and sobbed her anguish over her dead son.

It had been long centuries before the evil that Eloen had instilled in them bled away, but it had. Born of a pure Dokka'lfar mother and my son, they had eventually turned to the Ljo'sa'lfar path and their heritage. Some of my people still believed them to be tainted with that ancient curse. The killing instinct runs in my family and I have learned to accept it over the long years. It has stood the test of time well and has provided a peaceful existence for all of the many races that lived under my rule. We now were spread over many of the parallel Earths and the commonwealth had proved to be successful. The humans under my control now lived a lifespan far greater than they had evolved to enjoy, and with that extended lifespan the tendency to violence had at last diminished.

Once I had an infected host to interrogate again, I might be able to infiltrate the mind of the Collective without it knowing.

CHAPTER SEVEN

John Smith and Chisbolt had established themselves at Castle Haven. The goblin had placed a call to all his many relatives to get in contact and urge the ones who had helped to make safe the atomic weapons to make their way to the castle. John's descendants had settled at the castle with many of the humans that had left the dying Earth and had established a university of a combination of elfin, goblin and human sciences. All kinds of children were taught at the schools from every background of species. Trolls, gnomes and the dwarves sent their children to the schools as well, to be given a basic education and history of the multi-species. Those amongst them that excelled were automatically enrolled into the university and some eventually taught there. Mental science was taught to those who were talented in this field.

The great challenge of the time was the integration of the intelligent dinosaurs into the mix. Their mouths and throats were not adapted to form words; only whistles, hisses and chirrups could be uttered. So the elves concentrated on genetically altering the shapes of their mouths, adding an opposable thumb and a telepathic ability. It had taken centuries and a degree of ruthlessness by the raptors to achieve the fundamental changes that had taken their species into a greater realm of intelligence.

They had been integrated into the multispecies society to

the extent that they had been allocated a Spellbinder of their own to explore the parallel Earths. Vinr was the apex of their society and would one day be their leader. Now she had stumbled onto a threat to the whole civilisation Peterkin had put together. John now had the task of retrieving the weapons that the High King had made sure would not see the light of day again, except in some unforeseen emergency. Fortunately he had been involved in the decommissioning of the weapons and had a clear memory of all that he had done to make them safe. This he could pass on to the goblins and humans, by telepathically inserting those memories into the engineers he would be taking with him. They would have to check that each mechanism was in perfect working order before the plutonium was inserted. One wrong step and they would be vaporised when the bombs were dropped, taking the Spellbinder with them.

Chisbolt Hungry-face had spent many hours in his Spellbinder, feeding the knowledge of how to travel through the granite foundations of Castle Haven into his mind. It took a great deal of mental effort to undo the mental blocks that Peterkin had installed in all Spellbinders to prevent anyone unauthorised from entering the tombs that lay far below the living quarters of the castle. This required the actual manipulation of the Rift system, and this was locked inside the copied mind of Deedlit which existed in every Spellbinder. Peterkin had installed a mental command buried inside the goblin's mind which would activate the sentient ship's recognition system to unlock that ability.

Should he make a wrong directing thought, the Spellbinder could materialise inside the solid granite before it entered the huge tomb located a mile down. The resulting explosion would lift the entire mountain and Castle Haven into oblivion. Once the vessel had translated to occupy the spaces between the atoms, it had to maintain that state for some time while it sank into the ground. It was a more than tricky manoeuvre to do this and required a strength of mind that could hold the minds of the Spellbinder to this single purpose. Chisbolt had spent the last century manipulating the Rifts and exploring the parallel Earths, so he was quite confident that he could do what the High King required. He had seen for himself the devastation that had been unleashed on the human's world by the use of these weapons. It terrified him that his ship would be the carrier of these engines of destruction, but the love and admiration he had for his High King would carry him through.

Soon a number of goblins had turned up with their own sets of tools, ready and willing to put the atomic weapons into working order along with humans from the university. John Smith then spent time instilling his memories into each member of the workforce of how he had taken the weapons apart and removed the plutonium. It would be a case of reverse engineering to put them back into working order. John could give very little information about how long this would take, so he allowed two weeks and then to return with what weapons they had.

The Halfling shuddered when he thought about what they had to do a mile underneath the castle. He had told the inhabitants about the plan and the risks that had to be taken. He had advised evacuation of the whole mountain as well as the castle, and had organised for the inhabitants to move. During the time he had gathered his workforce, most of the people had moved either by Spellbinder or by flying the castle Quetzalcoatlus away to where the raptors had their settlements. Many of the gnomes had elected to stay and make sure that there was plenty of food laid on for their return. John had argued with Razzmutt's grandson without the gnome giving an inch. Razzmandios ran all of the castle staff and was adamant that as the trolls had not moved out of the subterranean vaults along with the others, then he was sure that John and his crew would be coming back. Ellywick, his wife, was just as immoveable and stood by her husband's certainty that they would return without exploding the mountain underneath the castle.

Privately John was relieved that they felt that way and he had to agree that the trolls were never wrong, but he had to err on the side of caution, so he left them to organise things for their return. Now he had all the people he needed to carry out the High King's wishes, and there was little to gain by putting off the moment any longer.

He faced the group and asked, "Any questions before we go?"

The green heads of the goblins all shook in unison, while the humans did the same.

John smiled at the engineering experts who were suited up in anti-radiation cover-alls and said, "Follow Chisbolt into his Spellbinder and we can be on our way. We all know how dangerous this is going to be, so I have to ask if anyone has second thoughts about coming. Speak now and stay here."

The response was that everyone stood up and made their way to the Spellbinder. The bubble was currently anchored on the edge of the parapet that overlooked the mountain range that castle Haven was carved from. Chisbolt was already sat in the command chair and setting his mind into the discipline that would take the ship and its contents out of phase with the rest of the universe.

John made his way to the side of his friend and laid his hand upon the green, bald head. "When you are ready, old friend, I think that it is time to go" he said.

The goblin nodded and concentrated his will upon the gestalt mind at his control, rotating Deedlit to the lead. The

Spellbinder became a ball just large enough to carry the members of John's team and began to change the fabric of the entire ship including the flesh and blood members. Every atom and molecule twisted slightly so that the mass of the Spellbinder would slide between the immense spaces between the electrons orbiting the nucleus. They began to sink into the mountain, with Chisbolt providing the bridge between the reality shifting mechanism of the gestalt and the power of the Rifts. Peterkin had set a Rift directly over the ceiling of the tomb that would drop the Spellbinder into the chamber hollowed out of the mountain's roots. They had to find it by drifting through the granite, following a line of force only detectable by a Spellbinder out of phase with the rest of the universe.

The sweat was already trickling down the sides of the goblin's head and dripping off the bottom of his pointy ears. His spindly fingers drove the pointed nails of his hands into the palms. The mind of Deedlit was keeping the very fabric of the ship tilted under the constant set of willed instructions from Chisbolt. The rest of the minds that comprised the gestalt sought the line of force that led to the Rift above the chamber and locked onto it. The occupants of the Spellbinder could see two scenes at the same time. They could see each other, but they could also see the material of the mountain as they sank through it. Sometime a large inclusion would pass through the vessel, as well as passing through the flesh and blood of the members of the team. This was very unnerving to the occupants. An occasional collision would happen as an odd atom struck a random molecule inside a flesh and blood traveller. When this happened in the eye, a tiny flare would fill the vision for a second. Should Chisbolt lose concentration for an instant, this flare would be magnified by billions and take the top of the mountain clear off.

There was a sudden lurch as the Spellbinder dropped through the Rift and into the tomb. Chisbolt altered the vessel and its occupants back into the reality of the universe they lived in and settled onto the floor.

The goblin stared at the bloody marks in his palms and said, "I feel like shit! I'm not doing that again unless I really have to. I'll use the Rift above us to twist ourselves straight out of this mountain and into orbit."

"Rest, old friend while I switch on the lights," John replied and switched on his torch and walked outside.

The first things that struck him were the cold and the moisture in the air. It had been a quite dry atmosphere in the massive chamber when he had been here before. The length of time had not given him any thoughts that this might present problems. The extraordinarily extended lifespan he had inherited from Peterkin's blood in this second lifetime had been something that he had grown into and accepted. There had been so much to learn and study during the hundreds of years spent at the university that the time had flown by. He had married a human woman and they had raised children, grandchildren and great grandchildren. He had not aged over those years, but they had.

Now humans lived much longer lives, due to the elves' interest in genetic engineering. The six Halflings and Mellitus had stayed together as a group, living together on and off. It had hit them all hard when Spencer had voluntarily followed the High King's mother in death. They had all been there when he had sung the Dirge of un-being and died with her. He had loved and been loved for century after century by the elfin queen. 'Dawn's Early Silver Light' had been the mind that had manipulated her son to take over the Ljo'sa'lfar kingdom from the corrupt Waldwick and defeat the Dokka'lfar by using methods that the elves would never had considered. Peterkin and his line were bred in their genes to have the ability to kill when necessary.

John Smith was an academic who had served the human armies in weapons development and military science in his first life. Now those ancient skills were once more being put to use by his friend and leader. It was not something that he relished and he was glad that it would not be his decision to activate the slumbering cargoes of death. The members of the activation team had strung out batteries of lights all along the vast cavern walls so that the whole tomb was illuminated. The air was stale and had a bitter taste about it. This far underground, there was no way that fresh air could enter and they had brought with them CO_2 scrubbers to prevent carbon-dioxide from mounting up and sending them all to eternal sleep. Two of the goblins were in charge of these vital machines and maintained them throughout the time they would be down there. The lights cast hard shadows which made all the team uneasy in the dead atmosphere of the chamber. There were occasional stains on the walls where bacteria brought into the tomb centuries ago had struggled to live in the dark isolation.

Already the teams had allocated different tunnels to check by Geiger counter that the plutonium-239 was still potent enough to do the job. Each lead-lined box had an access portal that could be slid open, facing away from the operator. There was little to worry about, as the deadly substance had a half-life of about 24,000 years. It would take hundreds of thousands of years before it decayed completely. Around each box was a layer of elf-stone that was immensely hard and also radiation resistant. Some of the boxes were warm and giving off a Cerenkov glow, and these tunnels were hurriedly evacuated by the discoverers.

The next problem came to light when the team began to

check the mechanisms inside the bomb-housings. John was called over by one of the goblins to show him the problem. During the centuries all the oil had evaporated away from the sliding mechanisms, and in the moist atmosphere items had corroded. The atomic weapons on Earth had always been maintained periodically by trained technicians to make sure that all moving parts still functioned. Now, due to Peterkin's insistence on maintaining a weapons embargo, there were no back-up systems in place on any of the settled parallel Earths.

For over a week, the team examined the mechanisms of forty atomic bombs and found that in all of them the stainless steel sliding parts had become cold-welded together during the centuries that they had lain down underneath Castle Haven. None of them could be made to safely operate, even when penetrating oil was used. John came to a decision and called the company together, as already the air was beginning to have a distinct foulness to it as the scrubbers on the CO^2 had begun to reach their maximum soaking ability. Ten of the forty tunnels had been signed as off-limits because of leaking radiation. A mile of granite over the top of them would render them safe enough and time would do the rest.

John spoke to the team that had laboured down in the tomb. "Gentlemen, we have wasted enough time down in the bowels of the earth" he began. "This will not be our grave, if we get out of it quite soon. Nothing we could do will put these sleeping engines of death back to use. We no longer have the tools and technology to deal with the problems of centuries of neglect. I see no point in collecting the tools we brought with us, or anything else. Leave everything down here. I do not think that we will be coming this way again, so get rid of the overalls in case they have soaked up any radiation or contaminants, and return to the Spellbinder."

Once all the team had relocated inside the Spellbinder,

Chisbolt concentrated his mind and working with the other sentient facets of the Spellbinder's mind, he headed for the Rift positioned at the roof. He then relocated to a Rift high above the castle. He opened it up to the welcome fresh air as they descended to the parapet, letting the sunlight through the now-transparent roof bathe the people inside. He once more attached the bubble of the Spellbinder to the ramparts and allowed everyone to get off before he turned to the human-hybrid and said, "What now John?"

"I will have to see Mia and have her contact her father while I think of another way to aid Peterkin," John Smith answered grimly. "Can you organise the return of the castle inhabitants? At least we can have a decent meal. Give Razzmandios our thanks and get our team fed. A gnomish table of food will do much to dispel the misery of that awful chamber. Oh and Chis, wait for me at the table and leave me a space. I think we may be needed to take the Spellbinder out again, but first I have to eat!"

John settled his mind and reached out to the High King's daughter, Mia, finding her at Castle Homecoming on Alfheimr, where she had made her home. The ancestral home of the Ljo'sa'lfar was now bustling with life and had been restored to its former beauty. In the many centuries since the Dokka'lfar and Eloen had been defeated, this parallel Earth had been seeded with new life with a mixture of dinosaur and mammalian organisms. Forests had been regrown and crops planted with an agrarian lifestyle, supporting the small cities that were dotted about the almost empty world. Great rainforests now dominated the tropics, pumping out oxygen and straining out what poisons the dark elves had left behind them. Only the temperate zones were exploited and lived in by the many different races that had chosen to live here with the elves. Under their jurisdiction the whole planet prospered and a non-technical lifestyle prevailed. Peterkin had allowed very few weapons to be used above the level of the crossbow, as they were deemed unnecessary. Any disputes were settled by a ruling elfin magistrate, and his or her judgment was final. Now that the humans had a considerably longer lifespan, violence had disappeared from the scene.

Mia had just finished her evening meal when the thoughts of her old friend, John Smith, entered her mind. She listened intently as he explained what her father had asked him to do and the results of that drop beneath Castle Haven. She concentrated her mind and said, "There was absolutely nothing that you could do? Am I to tell my father that his last resort has been taken from him?"

"Dearest Mia, whatever I tried would have left the mechanisms in a state in which they could have jammed or ignited on board the carrying Spellbinder. Those old Earth weapons must lie there forever and slowly become inert. You must tell him that there may be another way that I am going to work on which may offer up an alternative solution. Meanwhile he will have to think of every possible alternative that comes to his mind. Tell him I will return with Chisbolt as soon as I can, but that could be a while. What I have in mind will take some planning and a finely-tuned mind."

Mia sat and thought about what the Halfling had said, then she reached out to Peterkin. This was difficult, as the velociraptor's ship had skipped through a large number of Rifts to reach this reality. She had to open many doors and hold them there while she probed through them. Finally she opened the Rift next to the frozen world and slipped into the mind of her younger brother, Barathon.

"Where is my father?" she asked.

The elf jumped as his elder sister urgently charged into his mind and stared around the Spellbinder through his eyes.

"Greetings, Mia. Thanks for the headache! Father is down on the planet below. Follow my link."

Mia disengaged from her brother and reached out to Peterkin.

"Father, are you there?"

My daughter's insistent thoughts spun into my mind with their usual abruptness. I could tell that she was bearing unhappy news, and listened as she relayed John Smith's report. The atomic weapons were stored as a last resort, and not being of a technical mind I had thought that they would have remained untouched by time. I remembered that John had doubted the devices would still function unless they had been periodically checked and maintained. I had hated those engines of death so much that I had not authorised him to do that, preferring that they slumber for ever. Well, my wishes had come to bear fruit. I would have to wait and see what my chief scientist had on his mind as an alternative.

I said goodbye to my daughter and directed my thoughts to the bottom of the hill, where my grandchildren lay in wait for the next sauropod's appearance with a rider. They were a well-disciplined team and had honed their abilities, each supporting the gestalt. Cethafin signalled to the others that a possible quarry was coming towards the ford. It was at least seventy tons of brachiosaurus with a raptor seated on the base of its neck. The ground shook with every footfall as the behemoth approached the base of the hill. The rider was oblivious to the four elves hidden with their Quetzalcoatlus at the base of the cliff.

Firovel, Brianna and Kellynn prepared a telekinetic net to catch the raptor as Cethafin slid his mind into the host's body without alerting the over-mind of the Collective. He rapidly became aware of the heart beating steadily and tracked the main artery that fed the brain. The elf pinched it almost shut and the raptor fell into a dreamless sleep. As she did so she slid to one side and began to fall the forty feet to the ground. The other three elves wound the telekinetic net around her and lowered her gently to the ground, while Cethafin made sure that the host remained asleep.

The sauropod continued to ford the river, obeying the last command that had directed its tiny brain. It would be some time before the beast deviated from the direction and start to feed. The hunger pains that the Collective had put to one side would soon take effect now that it was no longer dominated. It had not been infected by a seed and was solely being controlled by the raptor bridging the Collective's mind into the sauropod's nervous system. Already it was slowing down and had reached the other side of the river and started to strip the foliage from the nearby trees. Its head was over fifty feet from the ground and its legs were three feet in diameter. The tail was still on their side of the river and waved from side to side as the beast started to walk again towards another tree.

The raptor was still fast asleep, and Cethafin kept her that way while his brother and sisters lifted the raptor over the neck bump of the Quetzalcoatlus with the power of their minds. They threw a rope over the sleeping creature to secure her and once secure, Cethafin urged the flying reptile to spread its wings and take the double burden aloft. The beast was uneasy at the extra weight and needed extra urging from the three other elves. It spread its wings and flapped them hard to raise them into the sky. The three others gave it an extra telekinetic lift to get it aloft and once it had gained some height the Quetzalcoatlus was able to gain control and circle round to the top of the hill where I waited.

I looked towards Night Flower and she nodded her agreement that she could not foresee that anything overly dangerous was about to happen. The rest of my friends made a perimeter around the top of the hill and had taken the safeties off their weapons. They were also broadcasting the message of 'not food' to the circling pterodactyls that had spotted the number of Quetzalcoatlus that we had pressed into service. Although our mounts were much bigger than them, they were adept at stealing food from the larger reptiles and to see a group together usually meant food scattered about. The problem was that the circling flock was enticing others to join them in a probable feast.

Reluctantly I gave the order, "Thin them out with a single shot so that they drop away from the top of the hill. Be economical with the bullets! What we have will have to do until we re-join the Spellbinder."

The AK-47s were powerful enough to drop a pterodactyl and even pass through them and take out two with one shot. Sam and the others held back until an opportunity presented itself and shot into the flock. As the flying lizards dropped out of the sky they were rapidly followed to the ground by the cannibalistic members of the group. Soon a feeding frenzy took over as the pterodactyls squabbled over the dead and dying lizards.

I watched as Cethafin executed a landing with his burden, unknotted the ropes and allowed the raptor to slide down the lower neck of his Quetzalcoatlus to my feet. My grandchildren lifted the unconscious raptor with the power of their combined minds and laid her on her side upon a usefully table-sized rock. This gave me the chance to examine the growth that was sprouting from the base of her skull. A lump the size of my fist had attached itself through the skin. A stalk projected from this growth and a mass of feathery fronds erupted from the end.

Vinr approached the sleeping raptor and said, "She is exactly like the other one we spoke to. The mind of this one, however, is more advanced than that of the first. I can feel that she has a coherent language and has lived in an advanced society. Her sleeping mind has more complexity and I can recognise many similarities to my own people."

I was pleased that Vinr was able to slip into the raptor's thoughts so easily. Generations of genetic engineering had brought fruition of telepathic senses. I had made contact with Prime centuries ago and found her mind quick to understand. This raptor would one day lead her people, if I could sort out this strange organism and halt its sway of dominance.

I slipped into the sleeping raptor's mind and with Vinr's assistance found the language centres and memories of the creature. I could see the life she led before the invasion of the seeds and her life afterwards. There was an immediate difference. There was less danger now as the majority of the big meat-eaters were now under the control of the Collective and there was an aura of control over this world. Free will had gone, but in its place was a kind of stability. I needed to know much more about this alien life-form before I made any hasty decisions.

CHAPTER EIGHT

The Collective had instigated the beginnings of the Quickening. For the very first time it was orchestrating hundreds of Quickenings all over this planet. Every continent that was large enough would be home to several sites. It had received enough information about the tectonic plates of this world to avoid rooting over a join. Now it drove the herds towards the rooting place. This world teemed with life and the larger animals like the giant sauropods were almost mindless and easy to control. They massed over fifty tons of meat and bones and there were herds that numbered in thousands scattered over the plains. Those of them that were hosts to the seeds walked, ate from the tops of trees and encouraged the other members of the herds to travel in the same direction. Those that died along the way provided plenty of food for the many meat-eaters that were also heading in the same direction. Many of the other herds of vegetarians also trod the same path, eating from the crushed and toppled trees that lay in the wake of the giants.

The greatest prize of all were the intelligent velociraptors which had become hosts to the Collective, as they had unwittingly supplied the stimulus to the alien creature's mind. All other worlds that the alien had dominated had been much more primitive planets and had offered very little in mental enhancement. Up until now the Collective had operated on instinct and memories of previous dominations. It had awoken as from darkness and idiocy to a growing sapience. Now it sent the velociraptors to seek out any host that was useless to its new purpose, remove the growth from the creature's spinal cord and implant it into another velociraptor's neck. This always killed the host, but the raptors gained a meal and the Collective gained another mind. Once they were implanted, the alien drew them into its neural net and passed on the ability of telepathy to each host. This enabled them to easily control any of the dinosaurs of which they had once lived in fear, and any of the vegetarian behemoths.

When the velociraptors demonstrated the use of fire and cooked their meat over the flames, the Collective discovered the sensation of taste. This too was a new thing for the rising intelligence to enjoy. As long as nothing interfered with the continual plodding forward of the herds, the alien did not obstruct the hosts in their day-to-day life. It also began to enjoy the feelings that were relayed back to its group mind from the multitude of hosts. When the raptors mated, the growing intelligence felt the pleasure that this brought to each individual host. This too was a new sensation. The Collective now existed all around this world, living inside many creatures, and it had a purpose - to survive at any cost. This new existence, with the ability to think and to be aware of itself was precious beyond anything else and would be fiercely protected.

Soon it would be rooted into the planet itself and then it would be secure. No more would it exist as a single rooted tree to dominate a world. There would be hundreds of its kind, each one a clone and another facet of itself. Once it had understood the strange thing that it had experienced when the object full of independent minds had lifted from the planet, it would apply that action for its own use with perhaps another seeding. This too would be a new thing to contemplate.

Most of all, was this new thing in the sky a threat? The Collective researched its memories of the many other planets it had dominated for many millions of years, searching for anything similar to the events that had taken place here. It had no sense of time as a measurement. Each seeding had taken place just before a catastrophe would have destroyed the alien life-form. This usually took place immediately before a tectonic plate ruptured and volcanic action took place. Until that time came there was no need to blossom and seed, wasting energy. It had dominated many different worlds, but none that had intelligent creatures which were altering their environment to suit themselves. Its level of awareness had been sufficient to allow it to bend the ecosystem to benefit itself, and although it had a strong sense of identity, its mind was now achieving a new level of understanding.

Its mind was aware that high above this world there were two objects that it could not understand which had independent minds inside them. It had caught a glimpse of mental traffic between the inhabitants, but most of it was beyond the Collectives' understanding. Once its seeds had been discarded, no more strange information came its way. Should one of these things come down and rest once more upon its territory, it would know instantly, as the entire world was full of eyes that relayed what they saw to the central intelligence. The trouble was, there was so much to see and understand.

I approached the unconscious velociraptor again and stared at the growth that was attached to the raptor's neck just behind the back of its head. The outside of the growth seemed to be quite hard; similar to a shell. The weight of my iron torc reminded me that to all purposes we were deaf and dumb to the telepathic powers of this alien being controlling the dinosaurs. What I needed to do was to loosen the grip of the iron band so that I could enter via the seed on the raptor's neck and unobtrusively gain entrance into the alien's mind. To do this I would lay my bare hands upon the growth and risk that I would not become attached. I instructed my granddaughter, Kellynn, that if that should happen she should strip the skin from the palms of my hands to sever the link. Meanwhile Cethafin would keep the raptor asleep and if necessary kill her to prevent the alien presence from realising what we were about to do.

Ameela linked to my mind as an anchor, to secure a way out should I get enmeshed in the alien's mental processes. My granddaughters linked into Ameela to store what information I could retrieve. Firovel maintained a mental watch over the area around the hill, in case any of the hosted raptors noticed the group hidden at the top of the hill. He would then make them forget if necessary.

I concentrated my thoughts into a thin thread and slid into the over-mind via the edge of the unconscious raptor. I became a minute speck in a mind which, I suddenly became aware, was distributed all over this world. There were millions of connections spread throughout many different life-forms, but the majority of the hosts were the intelligent velociraptors. Every host at the moment was involved in something that the over-mind referred to as the Quickening. This was the gathering together that we had witnessed which had the herds moving to a central area. The over-mind was a collective gestalt made up of all the minds under its control. It was able to use any living creature as a host to carry its seeds and minister to the Collective's needs. There was a central intelligence which relied on the additional identities of the hosts to expand its consciousness.

The more I allowed the workings of this mind to seep into

my own, the more I began to realise that the age of this alien organism went back hundreds of millions of years. It had changed worlds many times, sending its seeds out into deep space to dominate a new world. This was the first time it had encountered intelligent life, and its mind had blossomed. Up until this seeding, the Collective mind had worked mainly on instinct. Now it had become awake in a manner that had changed its consciousness forever.

I became aware that the fleeting meshing of minds had left ghost memories of Vinr and Nuzac behind. The alien mind now knew of the existence of my commonwealth, and if it could understand the manipulation of the Rifts, there was nothing to stop it seeding the parallel Earths.

I suddenly realised what the Quickening meant. It was the re-creating of the stationary stage of the Collective which became the Tree that produced the seeds. This was what I had to stop at all costs. We would have to follow the herds to the central 'sprouting site' and decide what to do to abort the growing tree. One atomic device would have done the trick, but this was not to be. Mia had been quite certain that my loyal friend John was unable to get any of those engines of death to work and he was investigating another method of destruction.

Whilst I was busily extracting more knowledge, I felt Cethafin tire and slightly release his light grip on the main artery into the raptor's brain. For a fraction of a second the host's mind surfaced, and immediately I felt an answering power reach out. It touched my cognizance briefly and the emotion I received was a burning curiosity about us, coupled with the need to survive at all costs. It now knew that we were here on its world, but not where we were. I swiftly slipped an iron torc around the raptor's neck and buckled it shut.

"Release the raptor's mind from sleep, Cethafin, but be ready to restrain her when she wakes," I told him, and stepped back. Vinr put herself into full view so that the raptor would see her first, as something familiar. She made the raptor's sign for non-attack and displayed empty hands as the female opened her eyes. The host to the Collective stared back at Vinr and sat up, curling her tail behind her. She clutched at the torc around her neck and caught sight of the other members of my team. Vinr once again displayed empty hands to the captive female, which helped to calm her down.

Considering that the raptor had never seen an elf or Halfling before she took her awakening amazingly well. She chirruped and whistled a long series of inquisitive sounds at Vinr and pointed to us.

"Show empty hands," Vinr responded. We did so and the raptor visibly relaxed.

All of us could converse telepathically with the velociraptors, but the spoken language, with its chirrups and whistles, was impossible for our throats to imitate. Vinr had been taught our spoken language and had been genetically altered to be able to do so. This had taken many generations, but had proved successful. Leader of Ten had joined with the mind of our captive and had listened to her speech and learned much of her language, finding it similar to hers. As she spoke, the alert mind of the genetically-improved raptor interpreted the sounds their captive made and funnelled the meaning to my mind.

The raptor pointed to Nuzac and made another long series of sounds. Vinr interpreted, "She says that 'We' have seen this creature before. What are you? Why can I not hear 'the voice that tells'?"

I deflected that question by saying, "Ask her where she was going with the huge beast and why?"

Before Vinr could ask that question, the female suddenly became aware of the iron collar that she was wearing around her neck and reached for it. Cethafin reached out with his mind and stopped her from touching it by making her lower her arms. Her eyes opened wide with fright and she started to struggle and tried to fight the telekinetic grip that my grandson had upon her. Realising that he was only adding to the problem, he reached into her body and pinched the carotid artery almost closed to send her back to sleep. Her eyes soon closed and she slumped to the stony ground.

With the iron collar around her neck the alien organism could not sense her or look through her eyes and ears. I could use my augmented telepathic powers and slip into her mind as long as I maintained physical contact with the raptor. I checked the security of the collar and made sure that she would not be able to undo the clasp. She was my bridge to the creature that was dominating the life-forms on this world. Most important, she would be able to direct us in the general direction of where the 'Quickening' would take place. I needed her to be awake.

"Cethafin, let her return to consciousness," I ordered, "but slowly. Just make her limbs heavy. I am satisfied that she will not be able to remove the collar as the buckle would require thumbs to do this. She has none, unlike Vinr. Use the lightest of touches upon her. I do not want her terrified. Do you understand?"

"Yes grandfather," Cethafin replied and eased the pressure on the artery into the raptor's brain. Once again the raptor regained consciousness and as her eyes opened, Vinr made the sign of empty hands in front of her face. The possessed creature stared back warily and climbed to her feet. She gazed at all the unfamiliar creatures around her, taking in the fact that we were controlling the flying beasts just as she had been controlling the huge sauropod before we had taken her off the beast. She uttered a number of whistles and chirrups to Vinr and waited.

Vinr nodded to the female and said, "She wants to know who and what we are, Peterkin, and what is it we want."

"Tell her that we have come from another place like this. We have come to stop the Collective from dominating this world and ours," I replied. "Ask her where she was taking the giant beast and why."

Vinr answered the raptor in her own version of the speech the raptors used and held the other's hand in hers, so that she could also read her mind.

Turning from the captive, Vinr said, "She asks why you should want to stop the Collective from organising this world and yours. She says that life here is better now that the 'Eaters' are under control. The 'voice that tells' requires the giant beasts to walk to a central point. We do not know why. It is enough that it is required."

That piece of knowledge shook me rigid. It was another viewpoint I had never considered; that the arrival of this alien organism would be beneficial. It would certainly not be beneficial to our commonwealth of worlds. It still needed to be stopped. I knew that all of my people would not take readily to losing their free will. I certainly would not easily give up my wardenship of everything I had built up with my people.

"No," I thought, "this alien life-form had to be stopped here on this world. How to do that would not be easy!"

Somehow I needed to gain the Collective's confidence and lull it into accepting that we were not a threat. To do that I needed to be able to converse with it, and that meant removing the iron torc from the raptor's neck. The problem was that the Voice that Tells would know where we were the moment that we did that. It was risky, but I could see no alternative. I passed on my intentions to my grandchildren and we discussed the alternatives and found none, so Cethafin released the raptor from her collar and allowed it to drop from her neck. At the same instant we all relaxed the iron collars we wore and formed a mental shield, joining each of us to the other in a cascade sequence. Any attempt to strike out at any of us would be deflected to the next mind in the link. Each of my grandchildren had spun a mental web to the other and spread the net to include all the other members of the team. I put myself forwards as the receiver and contact.

We did not have to wait long, as the raptor stiffened and stared at each one of us in turn. We instantly realised that the Collective was with us. We simultaneously projected the attitude of 'empty hands' to the intelligence that was controlling the raptor.

The Collective understood the gesture of non-violence that we projected. I offered a bridge to the mind controlling its host. As I had done many times before, I offered my abilities with language and transferred knowledge of the elfin communication to this alien being. The raptor sagged as the Collective retreated from its host to assess the gift I had transferred.

"I have been instructed that the voice that tells will return. It has much to consider," the raptor told me.

I turned to the others and said, "Build a fire and call something suitable for food. Our mounts will need feeding as well as ourselves. Maintain the shield at all costs. We have yet to establish a proper dialogue with this creature. The less it knows about our intentions if forced, the better. Granddaughters, Brianna and Kellynn, I want you to wear the iron collars, just in case we need someone outside the creature's influence."

Night began to fall and we were glad of the fire. Cethafin 'called' a young iguanodon to climb the slopes of the hill and stopped its heart within reach of our mentally-tethered

Quetzalcoatlus. He opened it up with a telekinetic slice and removed a hind leg from the carcass to roast over our fire. The rest was broken open so that the beaks of our flying steeds could strip the flesh and guts from the dinosaur.

Sam Pitts organised a watch amongst the other Halflings. We could then get to sleep without casting our minds into the darkness continually for meat-eaters climbing the hill for the scraps left by the Quetzalcoatlus after their feeding frenzy. Fortunately there was plenty of dried wood to keep the fire going.

While the flames danced and scattered shadows, Ameela and I drifted off to sleep, watched over by my friends. My grandchildren had also settled down and dropped off to sleep. I could not forget that their other grandfather was Molock, the first Dokka'lfar and father to his accursed race. Yet I had managed to turn them from the dark path of hatred and killing to the Ljo'sa'lfar way of assessing the world. Eloen's poisonous 'pressing' of their minds had eventually evaporated and they had taken their places with me. Without those extra skills at my disposal I could never had dared to walk upon the soil of this world that now belonged to the Collective leaving the Spellbinder in the care of my twin sons, Barathon and Petronius.

Emerging from a troubled sleep, I sent my mind up and through the stratosphere to my alter ego orbiting far above me.

I asked, "Spellbinder, is there any word yet from John Smith?"

The sentient ship answered, "Nothing as yet, High King."

The loss of the atomic devices was the loss of an easy option. As my grandson had suggested, this was a purely Dokka'lfar solution to the problem, but unacceptable to me. Even if it was within my power, I could not leave this world a radioactive twin to the Earth.

CHAPTER EIGHT

As I looked around me, the morning mists were beginning to clear and my family and friends were stirring. I became aware that Ameela was watching me, as she often did. She smiled.

"What now, High King? What are your plans for the morning?" she asked, rubbing the kinks out of her sides where she had slept on something lumpy.

I shrugged and replied, "We will make our way in the general direction towards which the raptor was traveling. First I think some breakfast would be welcome - and here is Hoatzin, with mugs of herbal tea and some cold roasted dino. Feast while you can, my love, as we shall have to take to the skies. Before that I shall try to contact the Collective and see if it can understand our method of communication."

Hoatzin offered us a collapsible mug of hot tea each and sat beside us while we drank and chewed. In his usual direct manner the Mexican Halfling came straight to the point and said, "What now, boss? So far none of the flyers have broken away, but it's getting harder to keep them under control without feeding them and there's not much left of the meal that Cethafin called to the top of the hill. We need to get them into the air and flying to occupy their tiny minds."

I looked up to see the two human-elf twins David and Steven already packing their gear away ready for the next journey. The sun had cut through the mists and the plains below were showing signs of waking life. I could see that several of the larger sauropods were plodding purposefully through the thick scrub and trees towards some as yet to be visible situation. I called the troll Night Flower to my side.

She stood towering over me, her black wavy hair covering her body from head to toe except for her face. Sam stood by her; he only came up to her nose. The bond between them had remained steady since they had first met during the dark days of Eloen and the isolation of her children.

She stooped over and cradled my face in her hands, stroked my antennae, and said, "I can feel nothing, High King, that needs to be feared. This part of the journey will give no problems that are life threatening. All I can tell you is that what you seek is in that direction." She pointed across the plains.

I became aware that the female raptor was staring at me and I cautiously opened my mind around the iron torc.

"Come. See. I wait. The little one knows where I am."

It was the voice of the Collective speaking for the first time, directly to my mind. The meanings were a little blurred, but understandable. I reached out for more information, but got nothing, and I realised that its attention was elsewhere. Trying to communicate with the alien was like knitting with fog. It was just not there. It would bring its scattered mind to bear when we arrived at our destination. We could be sure that we would achieve nothing sitting here on this hill-top.

I stood and held the mugs out to Hoatzin and said, "We are on our way. Put the raptor in front of me after I have mounted the flyer. She will lead the way and we will follow."

The Quetzalcoatlus were still gathered around the bones of the iguanodon, pecking at what scraps were left on the carcass. They needed a mental reinforcement to stand ready to receive their riders. There was a great deal of hissing and snapping of beaks as the reptiles tried to resist the subjugation, but the superior minds of their riders soon stopped that. One by one they stepped off the side of the hill and soared into the sky. Once they had gained height from the morning thermals, the great lizards could glide towards their destination.

At this point I found it impossible to imagine what we were about to see regarding the 'Tree' the Collective would form as its stationary growth. Apart from the seeds lodged into various dinosaurs, we had yet to find out what the final form was of this alien being that referred to itself as the Collective. From the brief contact I had experienced before I knew it would eventually turn into some kind of tree. What that actually meant had yet to be seen.

I urged my mount to the edge of the cliff and made sure that the raptor was secure in front of me. She pointed in the general direction of where we needed to fly and I 'pressed' the giant reptile to launch itself into the air. We dived down towards the ground and picked up speed before the beast fully opened its wings and caught a rising thermal that took us high into the air. Now the beast straightened its line of flight to follow the direction the host to the Collective had pointed to. The others followed my lead and a flight of 'dragons' began the next part of our journey. As we travelled, my mind wondered what my chief scientist, John Smith, was doing to aid our situation. I wondered what alternative he would come up with now that the nuclear option was out of the way.

CHAPTER NINE

John Smith had spent a great deal of time researching through the elfin archives before he found what he was looking for. What he wanted was Deedlit's crystal library concerning the operation of the Rifts and what he had discovered. He had an idea he needed to work out, and the answer to what he sought lay somewhere in the memory crystals stored by the ancient Ranzmut Boddywinkle for the time that the rightful High King was re-installed.

The human-elf hybrid held the crystal in his hands and let his mind float into Deedlit's understanding of the Rifts. He had abilities now that he could only have dreamed of when he was a human being. Wherever he had gone to after his death, this extraordinary existence as a Halfling had given him far more than an extension to his life. John had the inquiring mind of a scientist and with the elfin abilities of incredible memory and telepathy, he had travelled down paths that human scientists would never have had the time to pursue.

As the centuries had passed he had found many interesting things to study. Although he valued the friendship of his friends, which had brought him to the fateful step of joining Peterkin on his quest to rescue Ameela, he found the company of goblins easier. They too valued science and knowledge for its own sake. He had donated copies of his mind to many of the Spellbinders to give the exploration vessels that extra edge at solving problems. Now the raptors had found something outside anything the elves had ever had to come up against. Now that the atomic devices were totally useless, it was up to him to find another way of channelling power into a defensive weapon. What he had in mind was very dangerous and once more would require the assistance of his goblin friend, Chisbolt.

Having found the information he sought, John opened his mind to quest for his friend and let out a telepathic shout, "Chis?"

"I hear you, old friend. Where do we travel to now, the centre of the earth? No, been there, done that," he replied and chuckled. "I'm on the parapet with the Spellbinder ready to go, stuffing my face with gnome cooking before you take away my appetite."

John smiled, as he had heard the goblin moan before he risked his life on some venture or other. What John had in mind would test the goblin's mettle far more than their journey through the solid rock of Haven Mountain to the chamber of death far below. So he made his way up the stone staircase from the library, wondering just how he was going to explain to Chisbolt what he had in mind to try. It had never been done before, but John thought that it should be possible and if it was, it would unleash more power than an atomic missile.

He found the goblin sitting on the table finishing off a meat pie with his feet on a seat watching for him. He gave John a cheery wave as the Halfling came into sight and sent the rest of the pie down the hatch.

Wiping the crumbs from his green-tinged face, he dried the grease off his spindly fingers on his ear tufts and asked, "What now, old friend? Where do you want me to go?"

"I know that you have visited many parallel Earths by wending your way through the Rifts, so what I want to know is how far from this world have you travelled? Have you gone beyond orbit?" John asked.

"How far from orbit to you want to go?" the goblin replied, twisting his head to one side.

"For what I need to find out and try a test, the far side of the moon would be just about right."

Chisbolt sprang off the table and stood, looking up at the Halfling, and said, "It doesn't stop there, does it old friend? Tell me the other bit."

"When we are in orbit around the moon's far side, I am going to try and open a Rift from close to the sun and blast the moon's surface with its fiery breath. This should be for just a few seconds or so. I may need to do it several times to master the technique, so we also need an uninhabited Earth."

Chisbolt nearly lost his pie as he choked on the word 'technique' and staggered back in shock.

"What!" he cried. "You are going to do what? Open up a hole in the sun and use it as a giant flamethrower? John Smith, have you lost your mind? Apart from taking a Spellbinder completely out of the gravitational pull of this world and into pure vacuum - and that has not been done before - you want to open a Rift close to the sun?"

"I think it can be done, Chis. I have to try, as the High King may need the power I might be able to wield."

"It's the 'might' part of your sentence that gives me the shivers, old friend. I do not want to be too close to the opened Rift when the sun pours through," the goblin replied, pulling on his ear tufts.

"You are coming, then?" John asked, knowing full well that his friend would not hesitate to be there by his side.

Chisbolt regained some of his greenish pallor and grinned.

"Who else would wipe your arse if it goes wrong?"

"Any more of those pies left?" John asked, looking over the

table at the gnome who had come to check that all was in order.

"I will see what has come out of the ovens, Master John. I will return soon," the gnome answered and disappeared down the stairs to the kitchen.

"No immediate rush then, John," the goblin smiled and reached for a fruit bun.

"I intend to go on a full stomach. Whatever the High King is up to, I think I can eat before I risk my life again in his service!"

The gnome came back with a tray of pies and Chisbolt's crew sat down around the table and tucked into the pies and pastries the gnomes had provided. They had all listened in to the conversation between the Halfling and their goblin captain. In their fatalistic fashion, all of them would follow the Spellbinder's master wherever he thought to go. Not being there was to them unthinkable. If and when they got back they would celebrate with gnomish beer by the flagon-full. Till then they would stay sharp and lend their minds to whatever was required.

Once John had 'talked' to the composite mind of the Spellbinder and clearly briefed them on what he wanted them to do, the sentient ship cast off from the parapet and floated like a soap bubble in the air before vanishing from the universe that Haven existed in. Chisbolt channelled the energy of the Rifts to translate the Spellbinder through several major Rifts in the space-time continuum until they came out into orbit around a barren and volcanic Earth.

"I think this will do, old friend," the goblin stated. "We can't do any more damage here than this world has already done to itself."

John agreed and gave the order to lift away from the gravity well of the world below and cruise towards the moon's far side, avoiding any Rifts that lay between them. This took several days, and Chisbolt took the time to alter the outside of the vessel to a fine mirror finish. Now John searched for a suitable fault in space-time that rippled through the sun and exited somewhere close to the moon.

He linked with Deedlit and the other minds contained in the Spellbinder and prowled the emptiness of deep space looking for a fault. Finally he found one. What he had to do was to enter the Rift with his mind and give it a twist to funnel the nearest end into a spout. He also needed to estimate the time factor in leaving the Rift open. Having nothing to base his estimates on, he decided that five seconds for the first try would be plenty.

Chisbolt edged the craft away from the centre, put it into orbit over the poles and made ready to depart at speed if things went wrong. The rest of the crew gave their mental support to open a Rift by the side of the ship that opened over the north pole of the ruined Earth as insurance. John meshed minds with the Spellbinder and opened the Rift close to the sun.

Ninety-three million miles away the photosphere of the sun erupted into the rift, shifted through space-time and flowed out of the funnel John had twisted with his mind. It hit the moon and splayed out until it flowed around the edges for the five seconds that the Halfling had determined. Chisbolt and the crew had translated the Spellbinder through the 'panic' Rift and placed it in orbit around the Earth instantaneously.

"Well, that went well," observed Chisbolt sarcastically.

"Actually to do that at all was quite a feat" replied John. "Take the ship back to the original position and I'll try again. I'll cut the time down and the size of the exit funnel," he replied.

The goblin just stared at him, swallowed and nodded. The Spellbinder entered the local Rift and exited above the moon.

It had changed its appearance completely on the far side. There were no mountains at the centre, just a rapidly cooling bowl surrounded by a crater wall.

John stared down at what he had created and said, "The temperature at the business end of that flare must have topped a million Kelvin before we shut it off. Let's see if we can control the size of the funnel and make the rift smaller by the sun. I will also cut the time to one second. You ready, Chis?"

The goblin clutched the arms of his control chair and nodded, reaching out for the panic rift with his mind.

John did as he had explained, decreasing the size of the Rift by a factor of ten and squeezing the funnel tighter. Deedlit's copied mind reached out with John's to the rift that went through the corona, decreased the intake side and once more opened a hole in space-time.

This time there was no need for the Spellbinder to move as once again the flare bathed the moon in a white light, but in a much smaller area of several hundred miles across. John increased the time and narrowed the funnel, altering the intake to become smaller. The end result was an incandescent finger of light that appeared at the exit funnel of the manipulated Rift and vaporised several cubic miles of rock. By the time John was satisfied with the manipulation of the 'Sun-Rift', as he now called it, the moon's far side had a completely different geography.

Chisbolt sat back in the command chair and stared at the landscape below them in horror.

"It would take a human mind to come up with this!" he said. "John, this manipulation of the Rifts is a weapon beyond anything that anyone could imagine. Were it not for the High King's need and our whole civilization hanging on stopping this Collective from taking over our worlds and spreading through the multiverse, I would fly this Spellbinder into the sun to prevent anyone knowing about this weapon."

"My dear friend, I would agree, but if we cannot stop this alien creature from invading our way of life, we will spend the rest of eternity in servitude. We cannot make unknown what we have learned here and it is not our place to deny the High King the results of our labour. It will be his decision whether to use this weapon or not. When we arrive at the world that the Raptors discovered I shall immediately transfer the knowledge to the memory banks of the other Spellbinders so that whatever happens, some of us will return with this information about the manipulation of the Rifts," the Halfling stated. "We have no idea what the future may hold for us. As always, it is in the High King's hands."

The Quetzalcoatlus banked and caught another thermal, rising higher into the prehistoric skies. I stared down at the rolling landscape beneath me and thought about the accident that had brought the elfin and human worlds into being. In both cases the dinosaurs had been wiped out, allowing the mammals to exploit the vacant planet. Slight variations in evolution had brought different life forms to the fore. In my world a primate had developed wings from more primitive times to assist its range from tree to tree. In the human world a much heavier primate had made the leap into intelligence and had produced two distinct species. Mellitus was one of them. Her people were once Neanderthal and had been saved from extinction by our intervention during the time we had fled the Dokka'lfar. When we had left the Earth of the humans behind and relocated to Haven, we had taken them with us and they had settled the rim of the giant crater. We had built Castle Haven on the mountain in the centre and lived there for thousands of years before the Dokka'lfar found us again.

I had done the unthinkable and destroyed the Dark Elves by being as ruthless as them. I thought I had completely eradicated them from history, but I had missed a half-breed female that had risen up and struck at the roots of my family, taking my son as breeding material. Now the Dokka'lfar strain lived within my very family, as all of my grandchildren were descended from Molock, who had raped Eloen's human mother. My son had given his life-force to save hers and died in front of his mother. Consumed with grief, Ameela had seized her and slit her throat, killing her in front of her children. It had taken a few centuries of isolation to bring them back into the elfin kingdom, but eventually they had shed their mother's poison from their minds. They now took the long view and wholly supported my rule and added their powers of telekinesis to the gene pool of our people. That human trait of ruthlessness and determination to do what needed to be done was a family characteristic of my line. Very few elves had that killing attribute and needed a leader that could do so, to be able to follow.

My thoughts were cut short by Cethafin's mental shout: "What the hell is that?"

I moved to the side slightly to look past the reptile's long head and could see a black line that stretched into the clouds on the horizon. At this distance it was impossible to estimate its true size as there was nothing to measure it from. My passenger recognised it immediately and I realised that this was the fixed part of the Collective that would produce the seeds that attached themselves to the hosts. This was what the Quickening meant. As we flew closer we could see that the 'stalk' projected from a hill made of rotting dinosaurs which must have been a mile across and a hundred feet high at the centre.

This was why the great sauropods were all moving in this direction. They were fertilizer to germinate the seeds they carried. It was no wonder that the alien had done a seismic map of the area, because the root system to hold the trunk steady would have to go down for miles to anchor the mass of the tree.

I signalled to drop down onto another range of hills several miles from the trunk to evaluate the situation. The air was thick with scavenging reptiles as they dropped onto the feast laid before them and tore chunks of flesh from the corpses decaying into the ground. We urged our flyers to a flat area where a stream ran into a basin, before cascading over a cliff to the plains below. Even from here the smell could be tasted when you breathed.

"Release the flyers," I said. "This will do as an observation post to see what we are dealing with. There is plenty of wood, so I would suggest a bonfire to deter any meat-eaters wandering in our direction. Brianna and Kellynn, use the elf-stone and construct us living quarters using your abilities. The rest of you establish a safe perimeter while Cethafin and Firovel also use the elf-stone to make this area safe. I will survey what is going on closer to the Tree thing by hopping from mind to mind. Ameela will do the same."

My two granddaughters took out a cube of elf-stone each and placed them upon the granite outcrop. This was what my scientific friend John Smith called nanotechnology, but controlled by the telekinetic abilities of elves. The stone began to fizz and change shape as rooms began to hollow out of the naked rock, directed by the minds of my granddaughters. Windows took shape and also doors that would only admit a person our size, keeping undesirable creatures out. As Brianna concentrated on the inside of the shelter, her sister altered the outside to direct fresh water through a filter system and into troughs inside.

My two grandsons altered the landscape to suit, causing an impenetrable fence to rise out of the rocks with a sharp spike facing outwards to help deter unwelcome visitors. The elf-stones contained the keys to altering the molecular substance of whatever they touched to a very hard and tough stony material.

Mellitus cleaned and checked his M16 rifle, making sure that no pieces of grit had got into the mechanism. Night Flower had cast her mind forward and could see no immediate danger, so Sam Pitts and the other human-elf hybrids decided to take down some of the local 'livestock' to establish a meat-locker.

Hoatzin was the better 'caller' and fixed his eyes on an iguanodon that was on the edge of a small herd at the bottom of the cliffs. He sent his mind into the animal and gained control, easing it away from the herd. The message of greener food dominated its tiny brain and it began to make its way up the hill driven by an artificial hunger. When it began to falter as the going got steeper, Mellitus added his mind to the pressure and the beast began to climb with an extra effort. It was a young one, just a bit bigger than a horse, and would feed the company for several days if they could get it close enough. It pushed its head through the undergrowth and found that it was surrounded by strange creatures that it did not recognise as a threat.

Mellitus took an obsidian blade that was sharper than a scalpel, cut the beast's throat and it bled out onto the ground. They rapidly butchered the animal into parts small enough to carry and took them back to the now-constructed shelter. The smell of fresh blood soon alerted the local meat-eating dinosaurs and within minutes the carcass was covered in rat-sized raptors taking advantage before bigger ones climbed the hill to take their share.

Ameela and I sat down on a comfortably-shaped rock and cast our minds towards the hill of corpses to see what was going on, by looking through the eyes of the dinosaurs that were foraging amongst the rotting bodies. We took control of a scavenger each and scurried over a carpet of old flesh and bones towards the trunk, avoiding the competition. To my surprise the creature had good colour vision and I was able to see quite well through its senses.

I stared at the trunk of this alien tree in awe. The trunk rose out of the ground like a twisted black cliff, from out of a hill of bones. The individual seeds had germinated and wound themselves around each other like a giant beanstalk, fusing into the trunk. Quite some distance up, a ring of aerial roots spread out from the trunk and anchored into the earth on the edge of the bone pile. It was difficult to estimate the size of them as I was looking through an animal smaller than my usual size, but I estimated that the diameter of these root anchors must be at least five to ten times the outstretched length of the scavenger I was using.

I looked around for Ameela, who had inserted herself into another scavenger. She stood erect and pointed to the side, where one of our hosts had met an untimely end. What had killed it was a mystery, as it had been torn apart. Now that I knew what to look for I could see that other scavengers had died violently and their remains scattered.

This close to the trunk it was dark, silent and very dangerous. As I squatted amongst the hill of bones I realised that the trunk was something like half a mile in diameter and the top of the 'tree' was above cloud level. Leaves the size of football fields followed the arc of the sun and darkened the area under the tree in perpetual gloom. Water constantly trickled down the trunk and sank into the ground, washing the nutriment from out of the decaying dinosaurs. It was then that the thought occurred to me that this alien growth was influencing its own weather patterns far above the clouds, draining the moisture from them.

Something moved above me and I had a moment to dodge to one side as a tendril erupted from the anchor root, seeking my heat signature. I vacated the scavenger's mind just before another tendril wrapped itself around the dinosaur and ripped it in two with the aid of another. The remains were scattered over the hill of bones.

My next thought was for Ameela, but she had vacated her temporary host before I had been forced to move on. Obviously nothing was allowed too close to the trunk, and anything that did gave its nutriments to the tree.

Ameela stared at me ashen-faced and said, "I told you, Peterkin, that we would come up against something beyond anything we have faced before and I was right. How can we destroy something as huge as that?"

"I have faith in the scientific mind of my friend, John Smith. He is a weapons expert far beyond the elfin minds of my own people in engines of destruction. If there is a way of destroying that thing, John Smith will find a way. It knows that we are here. All we can do for the moment is to wait for it to get in contact with us. So far it does not see us as a threat and we must keep it that way until we are in a position to strike." I held her hands tightly in mine. "We have got this far, my dearest love. Night Flower has not foreseen any serious danger in the immediate future, so we can rest for a while."

Sam Pitts came over to us carrying two pieces of roast iguanodon wrapped in a large leaf. "Are you familiar with the human fairy tale of Jack and the Beanstalk, High King?" he asked.

I took the food from him and shook my head, handing a piece to Ameela. "No old friend" I replied. "I'm afraid that there are many books of human literature that are unknown to me. Is there something I should know that is revealed in this story?"

Sam laughed and said, "No High King, but in the story there

lived a feared giant at the top of the beanstalk and he was the enemy, not the growth itself. It was a story that was told to our children and the giant was defeated by Jack chopping the beanstalk down. Judging by what your mind is telling me about what you have seen, we will require an awfully large axe."

"There may be another way, friend Sam, but I have yet to think of it. That does not mean that there is none. I need to establish communication with this creature, and until then we must wait. Evening is creeping in and the shadows are extending. We will go inside our outpost and get some sleep. I will leave the security up to you and see you in the morning."

Ameela and I washed our hands in the steady stream of water that cascaded down the troughs that my grandchildren had built from the elf-stone and drank from out of collapsible mugs we had stowed away. We then walked inside the stronghold my granddaughters had designed and built to sleep soundly until morning. This time we had a level bed to sleep on without any stones, and amongst friends.

CHAPTER TEN

Morning dawned with a steady rain, but all the team were nice and dry. My grandchildren had modified the outside of our stronghold by extending a porch over the entrance, and underneath this the Halflings had built a fire. Water was boiling in a collapsible pot and an infusion of herbs had been added. Porridge of sorts had been made from our dehydrated stores and was bubbling in another pot pushed into the edge of the fire. Chunks of fresh fruit had been added to the mix by Cethafin and Firovel using their talents to detach them from the branches of the trees scattered around the slopes of the hill. They had obviously been awake and busy for some time.

Our captive sat quietly with Vinr and watched everything that went on. I tried a gentle probe at her mind and found it unoccupied. So far the Collective had left us alone on this hilltop. I had to ask myself, why? There had been no night attack to test our defences. Now that morning had dawned I would have thought that the alien would have made some effort to get in touch with its invaders. It seemed to be in no hurry.

The thought entered my head that I needed to get much closer to the alien being's static form to understand it more. As I stood up and looked towards the colossal trunk of the Collective I saw a herd of triceratops making their way across the plains. I quickly gathered my people together and outlined my plan. Those of us that could fly independently would make our way to the herd and press as many of the tank-like ceratopsians into service as were needed. The others, meantime, would 'call' their Quetzalcoatlus from wherever they had gone to feed and would follow us onto the vast plains below.

There was one problem, and that was the native velociraptor that had been our unwilling guide to where the Collective had taken root. This host to the alien creature had offered no trouble and had been a useful bridge to the mind of this organism. Any act of violence against this creature might alert the main intelligence of our hostile intent. At the moment it had offered no violent reaction to our arrival, and I wanted to keep it that way. As long as we overtly did no harm to its realm, then it would not register us as a threat.

"Vinr," I called. "Take this female down the hill and out of sight, so that she does not see us in flight. When she is at the bottom of the hill and making her own way through the shrub, double back to the top and mount your dragon with the others. Join us at the herd of triceratops and make sure no harm comes to her."

"It would be more sensible to kill her. Dead eyes see nothing," Vinr replied in her pragmatic way.

I returned her answer with a doubtful stare and said, "Do as I say young one. I do not want to alert the Collective to what violence it is possible for us to unleash. So far it has not reacted to our presence in a hostile manner. Your life in the future may depend on small acts of kindness done now."

With that, I left the two raptors together, made a last-moment check that I had everything needed and launched myself from off the hilltop and across the plains beneath us. I was soon joined by my grandchildren flying in box formation around Ameela and myself, all armed and ready to defend against any flying predators.

After about a mile we were closing in on the herd, so I sent my mind into a big bull triceratops and filled its simple mind with a desire to stop. As he was herd leader this caused the rest of the herd to slow down and feed on the ferny growth as the rest of my family dropped down. As we did not resemble any of the predators that usually stalked the herd, even those we had not 'pressed' took little notice of us as we climbed aboard these great chunks of muscle and bone. Tucked away behind the huge collar of bone that projected from the base of its head, we were almost invisible. We let the herd rest and feed, waiting for the Halflings, Nuzac the goblin and Vinr to catch up with us.

Soon there was a darkening of the sky as the flight of Quetzalcoatlus swooped overhead and dropped into a clearing. This alarmed the herd as these predatory reptiles often dined on the very young that were soon out of the egg. They rapidly formed a circle with horns projecting out to protect their young. The riders gave a mental push to get the ugly creatures into the air and away from the herd.

There was some hissing of displeasure from some who had spotted very young triceratops amongst the legs of the defensive ring. Hoatzin filled their tiny minds with the proximity of a T Rex and they all rushed into the air and scattered, flying in different directions. We opened the herd's defensive ring and my friends soon had a mount each. Once securely tucked behind the shield we could be on our way toward that black line that reached into the skies on the horizon.

Now that we were down on the plains and in contact with our beasts of burden, we all checked that our iron torcs were buckled securely. We needed to vanish from the mental reach of this alien life-form. We would be far too vulnerable amongst the massed herds that were making their way towards the root system.

Now and again we glimpsed one of the raptors that had been seeded, seated astride one of the giant sauropods as it ploughed through the ferns and trees, mashing anything in its way. Their tracks made them very easy to follow and the broken-down trees made for easy foraging for the triceratops, as they could reach the leaves with ease. Their small brains no longer registered us as something new as we sat behind the great shield that was part of the base of their skulls. To their tiny minds we were part of their lives now and had always been there,

Suddenly my ride, the herd leader, stopped and bellowed a challenge. All the other ceratopsians immediately formed a circle and stood shoulder to shoulder, horns facing out. The young ones wriggled into the middle of the herd and became silent in their fear.

Striding up the middle of the crushed pathway a T Rex came, swinging its huge head from side to side. It was hungry, but not foolhardy. A herd of triceratops formed in defence pattern would present too formidable a threat of sharp horns.

The meat-eater tilted its head up and gave out a roar that was answered from each side by a response. If we opened our collars to take control of the creatures, we would shine out like a mental beacon. Mellitus unshipped the M16, levered a shell from the magazine and took aim. He took out the top of the T Rex's head from the roof of its mouth and the creature dropped onto the crushed undergrowth. The noise of the single shot made the herd a little uneasy, but being in contact we could mentally control them even wearing the iron torcs.

My old friend fired again and took the second one through the chest, smashing its heart. The third one melted into the undergrowth for a short time and resurfaced by the side of the one without its brains. The smell of fresh blood was too much, and the T Rex began to feed on the leader of the group.

Tearing chunks from out of the creature's back and hind legs, it began to feast. Another much younger one edged towards the second beast Mellitus had dropped and began to feed on that one.

The herd began to edge away from this cannibalistic feast and left them to it. The last one to go was the bull I was sitting on, as he made sure that his herd had retreated safely away. He must have been thirty feet from his nose to the tip of his tail and over seven foot at the shoulder. I estimated him at somewhere around twelve tons in weight and felt very safe sat in front of his shoulders. I gave Mellitus a wave and signalled him to take the lead as I took up the position at the back of the herd.

Occasionally we would amble up a rise in the ground and I would catch sight of the black line soaring into the clouds that was the trunk of the Tree and the extended root system that anchored it to the ground. I still had no real idea of what I could do to bring this huge entity down and destroy it.

Nagging at the edge of my mind was the fact that the raptor that had been host to the mind of the Collective had been quite content to be the thing's servant, as it had made life better for her. I asked myself the question, servant or slave? Was there a difference? What I did know was that if this thing were to spread throughout the parallel universes and infect the worlds we had colonised, free will would disappear from our culture. Somehow I needed to contain the entity to this world or destroy it here and now. That would depend on what my human-elf hybrid managed to replace the atomic devices with. One thing I was certain of, and that was that John Smith would have found something that would aid me.

The Collective focused its mind upon the host that had travelled with the different types of intelligent life and was surprised to find that the raptor was alone. There were no traces of the creatures it had come to know as elves or the others who travelled with them. It opened its mind to seek for them and found that there were none of these much more powerful minds to connect to. It sent the raptor back on its tracks until it reached the shelter that had been hollowed out from the granite cliffs. It made the raptor wander around the stronghold and was unable to understand how such hollowing out could be done. The shelters the raptors lived in were made of wood and interwoven leaves. They had never constructed anything from stone, having occupied natural caves. It was fascinated by the running water cascading into the stone troughs and out into the hillside.

The canopy that had been extended from the rock-face showed that these creatures could command the very stone to do what they needed. It ran the velociraptor's memories back and listened to the conversations between the leader of this group of intelligent beings, with a greater understanding of the languages they used. It became obvious to the Collective that these creatures were somewhere down on the Great Plains, moving towards its static form. As yet they still did not seem to be a threat to its existence, and even if they did have strange powers that the Collective did not understand, the entity was willing to wait and see what they wanted.

It had noticed one strange thing on the way to the top of this hill, and that was the remains of the iguanodon scattered around an area that it would have not naturally climbed to. The Collective now understood a great deal of the ecology of this planet's wildlife and was learning to manage it, as it had done many worlds before. The presence of the remains pointed out that there must have been some kind of mental coercion applied to make it climb the hill to die. It had made contact with these strange intelligent beings before and its lack of knowledge of their abilities was a problem. They had some means of shutting off their minds so that it could not contact them or know precisely where they were. This had happened when its consciousness was concentrated on the other side of the world, tending to the many other parts of itself that had responded to the Quickening it had instigated. This was the first time it had reproduced itself in any numbers as other worlds it had dominated before had been mindless.

The Collective now realised since it had 'awakened' that it was able to soak up the intelligence of its hosts and employ that gift. It hungered for the acquisition of these new and far more intelligent beings to blend into its psyche. Once it could master the manipulation of the Rifts that had brought these creatures here, it could bloom and seed. If it could take just one of these beings and integrate it as part of its mind, and all of the multiverse would be the Collective's to spread into.

It returned its consciousness to the raptor at the shelter, only to find that it was at the point of death; the Collective had forgotten to release it and it was dying of thirst. The creature plunged her head into the trough and drank gratefully, but it was also starving hungry. Some roast meat had been left behind when the elves had gone and the raptor tore it to shreds and ate. The Collective left the raptor to its own devices and cast its mind further towards its static form, searching for other raptors that were urging the giant sauropods towards the root system. It could look through their eyes to find where the invaders had got to. The alien entity flowed from mind to mind through its 'herd keepers', searching for a host that might have a clear view - and finding one.

This particular Seismosaurus was around 120 feet long and 100 tons in weight and was the leader of the herd. Sitting behind the base of its skull was an intelligent raptor which had been the leader of its tribe. She was easily able to command the tiny brain of her huge mount now that she wore the

Collective's seed. She would be host to the seed until her extended lifespan came to an end. Once that happened the seed would be passed on to one of her grandchildren to become a new servant of the Tree. Only the seeds that had been ingested by the almost mindless dinosaurs had been allowed to germinate, once their hosts had died on the hill of bones. Now that the trunk of the Tree was settled and the decaying hill of dinosaurs had been established, there would be little need for another huge sacrifice for some time. This 100-ton creature would be among the last of its kind required to be used as fertiliser. When it died and added its flesh and bones to the pile, the Collective would selectively kill and cull the meat-eaters that came to feed on the carrion. It would also seek out those that preyed upon the animals the velociraptors needed to feed on. The smell of rotting meat would pull the carnivorous dinosaurs from twenty miles away, depending on the winds.

At the insistence of 'the voice that tells', the raptor stopped the great beast and made it rear its head high above the trees so that she could look back along the trail the huge sauropod had left through the flattened trees. Some miles back she could see a large herd of the horned beasts that her kind avoided due to their unpredictable temper. They were following the flattened plants feeding off them. In among the sprawling herd there was a group of the beasts keeping in a close formation, which seemed unusual. As none of the triceratops was host to a seed of the Collective, it was impossible for the alien entity to see any more than the raptor could from the head of the sauropod. With its new range of intelligence however, the alien was able to recognise the different behaviour within the herd.

The Collective probed the area and could not sense any of the powerful minds it had invited to meet it. The sauropod was getting close to the root system and would soon be offering itself up to the grasping tendrils which would wring the juices from its body. Soon the hosting raptor would be able to leave the beast to its fate and return to her village. On her way back she could spy on the Collective's visitors.

Content that the invaders were unaware of their approach being noted, the Collective swung its mind around to the internal workings of the main trunk of its static form. It was initiating the process that would produce flowers above the anchoring root system. By the time the invaders arrived to a closer proximity the buds would have opened and filled the area with scent. Normally this would only happen when it was time to expel its seeds from a world which was about to become unstable through volcanism or some other destructive force. With the moment fast approaching when it would fully understand how to open a Rift, the moment might well arise when it would be able to propel its seeds into a parallel universe and another world would come under its dominion. If it could find the world the invaders came from, it would increase its intelligence by the sum total of the inhabitants.

The rich nutrients provided by the huge sauropods and the other dinosaurs had produced far more growth than the Collective had ever experienced in its vast lifespan. With careful management of this world's ecology, huge amounts of nutrients could be called upon in the future. With its increased intelligence the alien organism had also increased the latent abilities that had lain dormant for hundreds of millions of years. It was confident that it would be able to control an infinite number of worlds by connecting through the Rifts and joining itself up into a multiple mind. With all the intelligent minds of the invading creature's home worlds bound to the Collective, it could spread throughout every galaxy, once every suitable parallel world was occupied.

On the night side of the world, what would have been called North and South America was the site of hundreds of the Collective's static tree-like growths. Around the rest of the world, wherever a suitable place had been found, the Collective had rooted. All across what would have been Europe, Africa, India and China, many more of the trees had held their growth back to remain hidden until the right moment. Here was where the majority of the Collective's mind was stored. It had learnt the expediency of diversifying its growth beyond the single tree that had always been the pattern in the past. To the Spellbinder in geosynchronous orbit over Europe, only the one tree was visible, and it was something that could not be missed.

My two sons were completely cut off from all communication with us by the fact that we all wore the iron collars around our necks. The only thing they knew was that we had landed safely and were travelling towards the giant tree-like organism that spread out into the sky below them. Since their elder sister, Mia, had informed them that the scientist John Smith had been unable to re-activate the atomic devices, Barathon and Petronius had merely kept the Spellbinder in geosynchronous orbit. They would have been happier if they had accompanied me, but fully understood that their nephews and nieces were of more use protecting me that themselves. They did not have the telekinetic talent that Eloen had passed down to her children. Anxiously they waited for news from their elder sister that John had indeed found something I could use against this alien organism. As the days had passed they had grown more concerned that he had found nothing, and then the mind of their elder sister broke into their thoughts and spoke with her customary directness.

"Brothers! Pay attention to what I have to say, as this takes a great deal of effort. John Smith is on his way back with

Chisbolt, bearing a weapon which is of such great destruction that it frightens him even to contemplate using it. In all the years I have known him, I have never seen him so fearful. He calls it the Breath of the Sun and his comments to me were that he wished in a way that he had never discovered it. Can you tell Father that he is on his way?"

"We cannot contact him, as they are all wearing iron to mask their thoughts. How long before he gets here?" asked Petronius.

Mia replied, "A matter of a few more days at most, I would imagine. Do you at least know where they are?"

"Not clearly, big sister," answered Barathon, "but the Spellbinder has tracked them through the terrain by their heat signatures. At the moment they are using a herd of triceratops to help mask them."

"What does our father think he will gain by risking his life and the others down there?"

"He says he will have a greater understanding of the alien organism if he can see first-hand what impact the Collective has had on the environment. The fate of the new intelligent raptors which are servants to that thing will be dependent on what he decides."

"If you need me, call and I will come. If you need anything I can bring it to you in a matter of days," she assured her two brothers, and switched her attention away.

The two elves joined the composite mind of the Spellbinder and concentrated on the heat signatures of myself and my team, monitoring our slow progress across the plains. Unknown to me, they were also concentrating on the manipulation of a small Rift that was now anchored at the shelter which had been engineered by Brianna and Kellynn. The twins had developed an affinity with this rent in space-time and had been able to move it around the plains below the hill-top. Each time they had moved it, they had become aware of its transitory nature, and they feared that it would evaporate and fade away. Their idea was that this could be used in an emergency to enable us to vacate in a hurry should it be necessary. Without the telepathic link they could not tell us this news until one of us removed the iron collar.

The triceratops continued to follow the huge sauropod, feeding on the crushed vegetation in the wake of its plodding bulk. We were now starting to approach one of the great anchoring roots of the two-mile-high Tree, so I called the small herd within the herd to stop. While the other ceratopsians continued to follow the huge beast munching on what had been the top juicy leaves of the overturned trees, we pulled back to watch. We all saw the velociraptor slide off the creature's small head as it lowered it to the ground. It then continued to lumber closer and closer to the nearest anchoring root while the raptor beat a hasty retreat.

The creature lifted its head to about fifty feet above the forest floor and something in the root system sensed that it was close enough. The root opened into a long slit and from this aperture erupted thick and supple tendrils which wound around the sauropod's neck and tail. The creature bellowed in fright and struggled, to no avail. A hundred tons of dinosaur was dragged closer to the anchoring root and crushed against the inflexible side by more of these powerful coils winding around the beast's body, until it burst open and spilled its intestines over the ground close to the root. While these tendrils choked the life from the beast, other tendrils thrust themselves into it and began to suck the fluids from inside. A human had once shown me a Venus fly trap which took extra nourishment from trapping flies. This huge dinosaur had just as little chance of getting away.

I had seen enough, and urged my mount to turn around

and move away from the deadly proximity to the anchoring root of the alien organism. I could see that other splits were opening along the length of the root as other tendrils emerged, seeking other prey. The triceratops needed little urging to retreat from this awful place, and we all urged our mounts to put on some speed.

I noticed that the raptor which had controlled the behemoth was making its way towards us unscathed by the spasmodic eruptions from the earth as more roots shot out, sensitive to the vibration of the herd. Some of the triceratops that had wandered too far towards the fresh green fronds trampled down by the sauropod were dragged down into the earth by the Collective.

We did not stop until we put a number of miles between the killing-ground we had spent so much time trying to reach. Even then we were unsure of our safety or how far the roots of this creature extended. The depleted herd began to slow down to a steady walk, and when it moved over an area that had large boulders and stone outcrops, I called for a stop.

I looked back along the line of our retreat and saw a lone triceratops making steady progress towards us. Unshipping a set of binoculars, I focused on the beast and saw quite plainly the raptor that had controlled the sauropod. It was making no attempt to conceal itself from us and sat in plain sight, not attempting to hide behind the large bony frill.

I could only guess that this was to be the favoured method of communication that the Collective was going to use to contact us. In that case I was determined that we would return to the stronghold my granddaughters had built. I now had a great deal to think about before I made contact with this powerful organism. I gave the group my instructions and urged the triceratops herd towards the hilltop that we had made our own.

CHAPTER ELEVEN

I watched the approach of the Collective's puppet with mixed feelings. Before it got anywhere near us I needed to speak with my sons. To be sure I would not be overheard, my grandchildren would put a mental fence around me to isolate my thoughts from the alien if it was trying to eavesdrop. The rest of the group would present telepathic chatter about preparing an evening meal and any other incongruous subjects they could invent.

I nodded and we all simultaneously removed the iron torcs from around our necks, ready to replace them in a split second. Immediately I felt the minds of my two sons reach out to me, and within moments they had told me Mia's news about John Smith's weapon and his imminent arrival. The fact that she had told them that he had perfected a weapon so dangerous that he was scared to use it worried me to my core. He had called it the Breath of the Sun and it was an elfin-based weapon more powerful than the atomic devices that the humans had used against each other. I could think of nothing that my people had ever produced that was of mass destructiveness. What he was bringing was a human and elf crossover of ideas. The humans had a way of adapting what could be peaceful knowledge to a warlike use, far more than even the Dokka'lfar could imagine. Their mechanical understanding was paralleled by the goblins, but it had a much darker side. Their history was full of endless conflict, unlike ours, until Molock was born and from him the Dokka'lfar.

They also told me of the anchored localised Rift which they had fixed in place at the back of the stronghold and said they could not be sure they could hold it there indefinitely. I thanked them for producing a bolt-hole and turned to my group and told them about it. Now that they knew, all of them could sense that the wall at the back of this hollowed-out shelter was different from the rest. There was a hole big enough for two people to go through, so I insisted that my Halflings go back to the Spellbinder, leaving just my family to wait for the velociraptor to make its way up the hill and into my presence. Sam and the others would have none of it, and they flatly refused to make a move until I and my family were safe.

We had all been humbled by the experience of being in the Collective's presence and its naked raw power. When the anchoring root split open and the tendrils seized a hundred tons of sauropod, dragging it off its feet, we all realised the power of the organism. It strangled the beast with ease and crushed the life out of it, sucking the body fluids until it was dry. The empty body had been cast off to decay and continue to feed the organism with nutrients as it broke down into the soil. Multiply this by the number of dinosaurs that were led into the traps by the velociraptors' hosts and it staggered my imagination to think of the life force this organism was draining from the land. If this creature was able to manipulate the Rifts and transport it seeds through space-time to the other parallel Earths, it would be the end of our commonwealth civilization. Whatever my loyal John Smith had discovered as a destructive force, I felt that it seemed more than possible that I would use it, but I had to communicate with this creature before I made any decision.

Hoatzin had worked his special skill and 'called' a number of leaf and nut eaters from the trees that grew around the stronghold. The others had gutted them. They had been skewered on sticks cut from the undergrowth and suspended over a fire. Soon the grease began to drip over the embers and they were cooked enough to eat. David and Steven had used the open Rift to slip back to the Spellbinder and pick up some extra supplies, including some sun-powered lights. There were other items that would have been too heavy to take down by parachute and wings. We at least could be far more comfortable while we waited for the arrival of the raptor that was carrying the seed of the Collective to become a bridge to the organism.

I called Sam Pitts and No'tt-mjool to my side.

"Night-flower, tell me what you see," I asked.

The Troll sat very quiet as she sent her mind forward. After a few moments she shuddered and opened her eyes wide, as if blinded by what she could see. The pupils had shrunk to dots and they streamed tears.

"There will be a blinding light," she declared. "Beyond that I cannot see. That does not mean that anyone of this group will die. I would know that, as there would be an 'emptiness' around anyone that would not be in the future."

I was satisfied that she had not seen the deaths of anyone in the group, but it seemed I would make the decision to unleash John Smith's weapon of mass destruction. I still needed to know why, so it was still inevitable that I would reach into the mind of this alien organism.

In the gathering darkness somewhere across the plains a velociraptor host to the Collective was steadily making its way towards me. There was a full moon and a strong silvery light illuminated the approach to the hill which we had adapted to our needs. By now the alien emissary would have abandoned the triceratops and would be making its way on foot up the hill towards us.

I called for Vinr and Nuzac to take a lamp, wait for the raptor's approach and guide the creature to where I was waiting. Ameela wiped the grease from her fingers and washed in the running water trough and I felt her mind inside mine.

"Whatever you decide, my Peterkin, you know that I will always be with you," she thought, opening herself to my scrutiny. "Night-flower has glimpsed the awful power that your resurrected friend is bringing to you. Although she says that none of us will die, I am still very much afraid. I have caught undertones from this alien thing. It is neither male nor female, but a combination of both. What possible common ground can we have with this thing?"

"We have seen the physical power of its static form. Can you imagine what that would do, if it rooted within the worlds we have settled? I have to find some way of stopping it or find a compromise that will benefit the both of our organisms. To do that, I have to link up with its mind and find out more about its aims and ambitions. I have to try and understand it somehow. I will need you as my anchor once more to prevent me getting lost inside its mind. My grandchildren will once more build a shield by being both connecting anchors and links back to my two sons at the Spellbinder."

Here again was a reservoir of strength that I could call upon if I needed it. The fact that we had done this before made the operation that much easier. Everyone fitted together as well as a hand in a soft leather glove and I was quite confident that we could make contact with this alien organism without anyone getting trapped inside it.

The Collective had managed a T Rex into shadowing the path of the triceratops to make sure that other meat-eaters would not attempt to challenge the beast, while its servant rode the solitary creature across the plains towards the hill. Once the velociraptor had dismounted the triceratops and made its way up the hill, the Collective had no further use for it and it would leave the T Rex to try its luck with the horned dinosaur.

A new emotion flooded the alien's mind, of anticipation and an impatience to merge minds with this superior life form. So much had changed since it had arrived on this planet in its appreciation of life. The eons of existence and managing the ecology of entire worlds were as nothing compared to this sudden upwelling of awareness and understanding. The Collective had demonstrated its power to the independent creatures that had come to this world to meet it, by allowing them to get close to its static form. All over this world its clones had rooted and were prepared for whatever outcome would be staged here. All of them had stayed their growth to remain underneath the canopy roof. This could change, the moment that the Collective decided otherwise. All of them were primed to flower and once fertilised to produce seeds that could be spread throughout the multiverse. All the Collective needed was a better understanding of the manipulation of the Rifts, and every time the elves used that knowledge, it learned a little more.

It was aware of a distortion in space-time where the creatures had made their temporary home. This had been used several times and had permitted traffic back and forth between the group of minds that hovered far above this world and the hill-top. The Collective considered this strange thing as it likened it to a giant seed-case that enabled the creatures within to travel between parallel universes. This notion that there were other worlds almost identical to this one just a 'doorway' away filled the Collective's mind with a hunger to know more. No longer would it need to travel the starry wastes for incredible lengths of time, once it fully understood how to use the elfin method of twisting a Rift to suit their purpose.

As it looked up the hill, it saw through the eyes of its host a brighter light than the silvery radiance of this planet's moon moving towards it. With this light was an organism similar to the one that hosted its seed and the creature that it now knew to be a goblin. They both beckoned to the female and showed the sign for empty hands. This the Collective understood as a symbol of a non-offensive situation. The raptor made her way up the hill and recognised the pathway the other host had travelled when the Collective had examined the site before. The raptor that had been here and made contact with the independent creatures had left to make her way back to her people. She was of no further use at the moment and the alien had let her return to her people.

Once the raptor got close enough, the Collective realised that the light they carried was not a flame, but a cold light that could be carried without burning the carrier. The alien filed this away as something different from the simple tools the raptors had produced. Now its new-found curiosity really began to ignite. What wonders it would soon have in its power to exploit and understand! The creatures it now knew as elves would make such superior hosts, along with the other exciting sentient creatures that lived with them.

I watched the progression of the light up the hillside with Ameela at my side and reviewed my plan of action. John Smith and Chisbolt had arrived while I awaited my emissary from the being that I now knew as the Collective. I now fully understood why he was so terrified of the power he had discovered. I had seen through his eyes what the Breath of the Sun could do when it was unleashed. I had shown him where the Tree had rooted and its position on the plains. I had warned the others that No'tt-mjool had foreseen that I would unleash this power as a last resort and that they must retreat through the Rift back to the Spellbinder as soon as it flared.

Once again my family built a cage around my mind to protect me as I prepared myself to dive into the mind of the Collective.

The light, the goblin and the two raptors turned the corner and I once more felt that I was in the presence of the alien being. Vinr offered the raptor a drink of fresh water, as we knew from past experience that the Collective tended to forget what fragile creatures its hosts could become. She drank gratefully from the mug that was offered and approached me.

I had undone the iron torc around my neck along with all the others and sent my mind into the puppet-master via the raptor's bridge.

"It is time we made proper contact," I insisted.

"Then blend your mind with mine and see what I see and experience," the vast mind of the Collective replied.

I became a multitude! Millions of eyes and ears swamped me with details and I felt the alien snatch parts of my mind and file the information away. I became the Collective and felt the awesome passage of time over which the organism had existed, tending world after world over millions and millions of years. It shared its awakening upon this world and the sudden flowering of self, beyond anything that it had experienced until this seeding. I felt its hungry ambition and the deep-seated urge to control all eco-systems. All sentient life would amalgamate with the mind of the Collective and by doing so change its state to omnipotence. The multiverse would become its playground as world after parallel world fell to its onslaught. There would be a managed time of plenty, but at what price? Free will would be a fleeting thing of the past as each new-born sentient being would be exposed to a seed on puberty. From then on they would be servants of the Collective until their dying day, which would be extended, while they were maintained in perfect health. Once it had absorbed the minds of the sentient races it would be unstoppable and would continue to expand throughout the multiverse, linking its vast mind throughout the Rifts.

I mentally struggled to escape from the grip of this eons-old thing and followed the thin thread back to Ameela. I slammed the iron torc shut around my neck to shut it out and said to my wife, "Tell John to unleash the weapon and tell the others to get out!"

On the Spellbinder that was piloted by Chisbolt Hungry-jaw, John Smith heard the order from Ameela that he was dreading. He reached out with the combined minds of the ship and his and twisted open a Rift next to the sun. He then joined that Rift to the one he had centred over the two-mile-high organism and opened that one into a funnel as he had done before to concentrate the 'Breath' on the one place for a few seconds.

Something that was far greater than his control took over and held the Rift open and widened it. The gravitational force proceeded to rip the ground apart as it turned into gas. The static form of the Collective vaporised and the mind control was disrupted. Frantically John managed to shut down the Rift at the sun and stopped the 'Breath' at its source, whilst suffering the mental scream of the burning Collective echoing through his mind as it shut down.

At the same time my grandchildren unravelled the telepathic web along with the others and quickly made their way towards the wall that contained the Rift. A bright light filled the room with an incandescent reflection as John opened a Rift into the sun and opened it over the position of the Tree. The pillar of fire unexpectedly widened and began to expand, traveling along the rotation of the Earth towards where we had made our temporary camp. It seemed that John had lost control of it and could not shut it down. Miles away, the rocks and the ground itself began to turn into gas as the sun consumed the parallel Earth and began to dig down to the mantle below.

Ameela and I were the last to hurl ourselves through the Rift towards the Spellbinder as John finally shut the 'Breath' down, the very air becoming too hot to breath. As this was done, the escape Rift moved. We abruptly found ourselves in sunshine. Luckily for us we had landed in a soft bush, some feet off the ground.

The next thing that pressed into my awareness was that Ameela was screaming in agony. Both her legs were gone just below the knees; they had been cauterised. We both had burn marks around our necks where the iron torc had welded shut and was still too hot to touch. The intense magnetic field had heated the iron up as we passed through the Rift and somehow we must have interacted with the closing of the other Rift above the Collective's static form. I had no idea where we were, except that as it was daylight, we must be on the other side of the world.

I quickly pushed my tunic in between my neck and the iron collar and reached out to Ameela. I held her in my arms and did the same for her, sharing the agony and getting it down to a bearable level by controlling the pain centres of her mind. Neither of us could communicate telepathically to anyone else due to the iron torcs welding shut. Somehow I needed to get them off so that we could transmit a cry for help.

No'tt-mjool was right in that no-one had died, but Ameela and I were as good as dead if we could not get help. This was after all, a dinosaur world and deadly to weak, frail creatures like us and with our long range telepathic abilities closed off we could not defend ourselves from the beasts that lived here.

The catatonic mind of the Collective had retreated to its clones situated all over the world. The pain that it had suffered when the elves' weapon had vaporised its first static form was beyond anything it had ever endured previously. Nothing had ever harmed it before in all its incredibly long life. It had never felt pain, as the nuclear explosion that propelled the seed-cases into the interstellar reaches was never remembered. Its memories of its past lives did not include the pain of destruction as it left all its previous selves behind. The Collective closed down into healing darkness and temporary un-being, releasing all the creatures that were hosts.

Barathon and Polonius had left the control chairs to stare paralysed with horror at the feet and lower legs of their mother, which lay where they had fallen when the Rift moved. No blood oozed from the stumps, as they were both cauterised.

Sam Pitts picked them up and demanded, "Prepare a stasis chamber, Barathon and place your mother's legs inside it. She is out there somewhere with your father on this world. Find out where the Rift has moved to and search for them. Move and take control of the situation! They must have the torcs around their necks, otherwise we would be able to hear their thoughts. Something welded them closed when John unleashed the weapon."

He opened his mind to his friend and asked, "What happened, John? Do you know?"

John was still reeling from the shock of losing control of the Breath of the Sun and tried to recount what happened.

"Something tried to take control of the Rift when I opened

it over that giant tree and opened it instead of closing it down. I shut the other end, but it took several long moments before I could re-establish control of the Rifts. Whatever it was did not die when the Tree was vaporised. For a brief moment I was aware that it was secreted all over the planet, and then it closed down. I cannot find it anywhere specific, but I do know that there are hundreds of the static forms, scattered all over this world. The Collective was cleverer than we thought and diversified from what it had done in the past. It has learnt the art of deceit and gained a subtle way of thinking beyond the simple form of life it enjoyed before it arrived here."

Sam turned to my sons and asked, "What are you going to do next? It would seem that the only way to defeat the Collective is to sterilize this world, and that includes destroying your parents along with everything else. This is something that you may have to consider. It is a High King decision that you may have to face."

Barathon reeled away from the Halfling and stared at his brother Petronius, the colour draining from his face. "We cannot destroy this world along with our parents!" he said. "We cannot sentence to death and non-existence a sentient race in the throes of evolving. There has to be another way!"

"Do not make any hasty decisions," said Night Flower. "I have scanned the near future and your parents life-signs endure on this world. They are not dead yet, so search for them. The future is not clear, as there are a myriad branches all with different outcomes. In all of them your parents seem to be alive, but there is something I cannot understand. When it becomes clear I will be able to tell you more, but until then, this is all I have."

Barathon and Petronius stared at the troll maiden with burgeoning hope. They full knew that the female trolls had the ability to 'look' ahead and that this ability had been used by their father in the defeat of Eloen.

"We have three Spellbinders hovering around this world. I think that Vinr and Nuzac should return to the raptor's ship and take Hoatzin, David and Steven, while John stays with Chisbolt. We will co-ordinate a search of this world and seek out wherever our parents have gone to and rescue them."

Thousands of miles away I was easing Ameela out of the bush and onto the ground. She had now full control of her body and was able to block off the searing pain of the cauterisation of her missing legs. I had examined them and showed Ameela the state of the stumps by letting her see through my eyes. They had been severed just below the knees. Fortunately for her, the cauterisation had prevented her from bleeding to death. Nevertheless it was impossible for her to move unaided. I would need to make a litter of some kind so that I could drag her to a place of safety.

There were no signs of any large animals near to us, so I left Ameela propped up against the trunk of the bush and scavenged for useful branches and vines. She had given me the obsidian knife that always hung around her neck on a leather thong. It was the very same knife she had used to slit Eloen's throat just before she had drained the life willingly given by my son to regain her youth. Fortunately we had landed in an area that was rich in bamboo of all kinds of thickness. I was soon able to uproot a couple of them and bind them into the classic 'A' frame, upon which I wove a seat for Ameela to sit on. I now had some means of dragging Ameela to a more defensible place.

I made my way back to where I had left her and checked her stumps. Already her elfin heritage had begun the start of the healing process by growing skin over the exposed area. She would heal underneath the cauterised area and eventually grow new feet and legs, but that would take some while. I had made her knife into a spear by lashing the stone to the split end of a bamboo stake, so at least we had some meagre protection. I rolled Ameela onto the seat on the 'A' frame and I wriggled myself into the harness over my neck and shoulders.

It took some effort, but I managed to finally stand erect and began to drag the travois down the hill and away from the bush. Soon we found ourselves on more open ground. Hopefully there might be water at the bottom of the slope. The surrounding vegetation was green and fresh looking, so I had hopes that there would be water somewhere near. My breath came in shuddering gasps as the effort of dragging the travois down the slope began to tell on me. In the end I could go no further and made for the shelter and shade of a large rock. To my relief the ground was damp and fresh water was oozing from the base of the rock. I wriggled out from the harness and lay for a while exhausted on my stomach.

Ameela stretched out her hand to touch my leg and I felt her in my mind.

"Rest for a while, my love. There is water here. I can see that there is a spring. Drink first as you have been the one sweating. You must rehydrate yourself. I will be fine sitting here. As you can feel, the pain in the stumps has diminished. I can be more useful now."

I crawled across to the base of the large rock and pressed my face into the shallow pool the spring had filled before it seeped away down the slope, and gratefully drank. I had in my pocket the collapsible mug I had used at the shelter my granddaughters had produced, and I filled it with fresh spring water for Ameela. I plastered some cooling mud over the burns on my neck where the hot iron torc had lifted the skin when it had welded shut. The burns would soon heal, unlike those of my human friends, who often had to endure weeks of healing before the skin would knit together.

CHAPTER TEN

I gave Ameela the mug of water and sat down beside her in the shade.

"What happened, Peterkin?" she asked as she sipped the water.

"The only answer must be that the Rift moved as we entered it. When John unleashed the Breath of the Sun it was only supposed to flare for a few seconds and was to be funnelled into a narrow beam. Instead of being contained, it broadened out and was operational for a lot longer than John had intended. Something took control from him and was unskilled at manipulating the Rifts. I think the Collective was responsible for what happened. I just hope we have destroyed the alien organism."

Ameela looked at me with a fearful expression. Then she pointed over my shoulder and shook her head. There, reaching up to the top of the canopy, was a large black trunk maybe ten to twenty miles away.

CHAPTER TWELVE

I sat paralysed with trepidation as I stared at that unmistakable dark shape in the far distance. All manner of thoughts raced through my mind as I sat there, stunned. How many more of the trees had rooted all over this world, I asked myself? We had been lured into a false sense of security in thinking that there would only be just the one static form of this totally alien creature. Now that it could think on a scale beyond its previous existence, it had reasoned that it might need more than one housing for its extended mind. No longer would this creature be satisfied with one massive trunk to house its intellect, it would need many to gather in as many minds to its central personality as there were velociraptors on this planet. Now it had dreams of empire. The more servants of the Collective there were, the stronger its intellect would be. What could it become if it added my people to its means? What would my sons decide to do once they were clear in their minds what kind of a threat this totally alien organism could do?

I pulled at the torc around my neck without it releasing. The catch that made the link had melted into itself and fused together. Looking at Ameela's I could see no hope there either, as the quick-release catch had turned into a molten blob. I did not have the ability my grandchildren had inherited from their mother of being able to reach into the molecular substance of any matter and scramble the very atoms inside it. They would have disrupted the metal in moments, cutting through the iron like a hot knife through butter.

Ameela broke through my thoughts and said, "I don't want to worry you more than I must, but we will need a fire if we are to survive the night. There will be meat-eaters that hunt in darkness, and without a fire we will be lunch."

"You are right, my love," I replied and got to my feet, ignoring the aches and pains of dragging the travois, to search for kindling and dead branches.

Once I had dragged as much as I could find around us I assembled the tools I would need. Mellitus had once shown me what to do with the bow-drill and tinder. He had insisted that I might one day need this skill and it could save my life. I sorted through the wood I had gathered and found what would do as a bow, anvil and drill. Like all elves I had perfect memory and recalled all of Mellitus' instructions. I wiped my sweat over the top of the drill to lubricate it and began to rotate the drill backwards and forwards, using the thong that held Ameela's knife holster around her neck.

It took some while before I began to see smoke rise from the hollow of the anvil, when Ameela quickly placed the tinder around the rotating drill. As she blew across the tinder more smoke began to rise, and I could see a coal glowing in the middle of the tinder. I snatched the ball of dried grass and fluff and blew even more. I was rewarded by small flames, which I dropped into the bowl of light combustible twigs and kept blowing. The ball of twigs burst into flames. I had the heart of the fire alight!

I added more broken branches until I had a steady fire which gave off a white acrid smoke. This would unnerve any of the many flesh eating dinosaurs in the vicinity. All we had to do was keep the fire going throughout the night. In the few hours of daylight left I was determined to scout around and see what I could find as food.

Ameela had managed to prop herself up to a sitting position and was surrounded by the dead branches that I had found. I had checked her stumps; they were free of any cuts, and the skin was thickening up somewhat. The one advantage we had was the healing properties that all elves were able to adapt to their bodies. All elfin blood was host to a strong mixture of antibodies which would prevent any infections from 'digging in', and that was why the virus, created by genetic engineering, destroyed the Dokka'lfar and spread through them, sterilising those it did not kill. It was a simple child's illness which had been altered to attack the Dark Elves that were mature. My mother had healed the wounds she had endured when Eloen had had her crucified, once the iron nails were removed. It was only at the point of her death that she lost control and had once again bled from the nail holes.

I used the point of the spear to probe into the undergrowth to find anything hiding and waiting for darkness. I heard an angry hiss from the base of a bush and probed a little more. A snake the length of my arm came wriggling out and reared up to strike. With a sideways blow, the scalpel sharp edge of Ameela's knife cut through the snake's body just under its head. I continued the decapitation, pressing into the springy ferns until the head came off. This I flicked away into the bush and moved carefully into the area the snake had emerged from. I saw a mound which could only mean one thing - a nest. Probing through the top layer, I could see that the eggs were fresh and had not been laid too long before.

I took off my tunic and tied the sleeves together, doing up the neck to make a carrying sack. Then I filled my tunic with the eggs, and carrying the snake at arm's length, I prevented the blood from staining my clothes.

I also stopped to gather some fruit from the bushes around our shelter and added them to the eggs. The sun was now getting lower in the sky and it would soon be dark. The smoke from the fire made it easy to get back to Ameela with my trophies. When I reached her she waved and said, "I have not been idle, my love. A large tortoise had the misfortune to wander too close to me and it now lies in the embers of the fire! What have you got in your shirt?"

"Snake eggs, quite fresh I believe, and also the snake that laid them. I don't think we will starve out here. What we have to do is to keep the fire going and hope that when they search for us, they see the smoke." I sat beside her.

"Help yourself to the tortoise, Peterkin" she laughed. It's been in the embers almost since you went foraging. Drag it out and pull off the legs, all this fresh air has made me hungry."

I removed the eggs from my tunic, redressed myself and put the snake in the embers of the fire to cook along with six of the eggs. The next thing I did was to remove the tortoise from its shell by smashing the underneath armour; then I cleaned it out. We now had a basin to allow the spring to fill once I had dug a hollow to fit it into. I filled my collapsible mug from this and offered Ameela a fresh drink. The heat of the fire had made the armoured skin easy to peel off and we soon tucked into the meat that lay underneath.

We could hear movement at the bottom of the hill as a herd of something congregated around the water hole into which the spring drained. Occasional grunts and squeals rang through the air as the creatures jostled for position to drink. I tossed some more branches on the fire, and as the flames climbed upwards, the beasts at the bottom of the hill responded by stampeding away in fear. As they did so there was a shriek of pain as a large meat-eater took one of the creatures out with a sideways charge. I responded to that by dragging a fallen log onto the fire and heaping up some more branches on the top of it.

Ameela put her hand upon my arm and entered my mind. "Stay quiet, my love and sleep" she said. "I will take first watch while you rest. There is plenty of wood I can reach, so lie down on the bed of ferns you gathered and rest."

I reached round, kissed her gently on her forehead and touched her antennae with mine, just as we had when we had first made love in the snow of Haven. I had lost my wings because of that moment of madness. Her father had sliced my wings from my back and sealed the stumps with hot irons. It had taken a long time for the healing ointment we took from Molock's castle to encourage regrowth. We had achieved so much since I had seized power from the maddened High King and built what was now a commonwealth of worlds, where the many sentient species of the parallel worlds lived. I would not easily let this alien creature take all that away from us.

I settled down into the ferns and soon slept the sleep of sheer exhaustion, the aches and pains of my extreme efforts forgotten.

Ameela shook me awake and I reluctantly surfaced and sat up.

"Is everything OK?" I asked and stretched my arms out to pick up some dry wood.

"It's been very quiet for some time, ever since the herd moved away," she said and burrowed into the warmth of my bed. "Wake me when the sun has broken through morning clouds. Not too early, my love! I too need to sleep and heal, although I must say that my pain has diminished. It will be a long time before I walk again, but I might be able to fly if you can think of some way of protecting my stumps when I land! Now I must sleep."

She pulled the ferns over her head and I covered her legs to keep her warm after I had fed some more branches to the fire. I sat and wondered what my sons and grandchildren were doing. John Smith had been proved right in his fear of the weapon he had discovered by using the manipulation of the Rifts. Whatever had happened, we had but a few moments to live or hurl ourselves through the Rift and back into the Spellbinder. Something must have interfered with John's control of the exit of the Breath of the Sun and it had to be the Collective that had done so. One thing was certain; the intelligence had not so far learnt to manipulate the Rifts with any certainty.

Somehow I had to break open one of these iron torcs that were welded shut around our necks. I tried once again to bend the torc out of shape and use metal fatigue to break it open, without any effect.

I watched the moon set, and it got dark and cold in the hours before the dawn so I built up the fire. Until this time I had been careful to eke out the wood I had collected, but now with the last hours of the night and the hunting reaching its end, I piled on the last of the wood. Now a thick mist began to creep up from the valley below and the smoke from the fire helped to reduce the visibility. I stood up and placed some more of the snake eggs I had gathered in the embers of the fire, covering them with hot ash. Already the sky was lightening to the east; soon the dawn would break.

This was a good place to camp, with fresh water nearby and still plenty of dead wood to be gathered. There was nowhere we could go to that would be any better than where we were, although it was poorly defended. I turned and watched my wife sleep quietly amongst the ferns. The sun began to climb into the sky and the cold of the night began to ease away. Neither of us had been dressed for going on safari, as all our protective clothing had been stored back on the Spellbinder. We had been lulled into a false sense of security by the Rift that my sons had anchored to the back of the shelter. All we had was what we stood up in and what we happened to have in the pockets of our tunics. Fortunately we at least had a sharp blade, which I had securely bound to the split end of a piece of stout bamboo. Ameela had carried that knife around her neck in a holster ever since her father had isolated her on the Tower of Absolom. She had cut Eloen's throat with it when she had drained the life from our first-born son. My grandchildren had been there and watched as their Dokka'lfar mother had drained her lifeblood into the ground with their grandmother's hand wound around Eloen's hair, holding her head back. It had taken centuries before all her poisonous mental conditioning had faded away. They were one eighth human by genetics and had all developed the latent power of telekinesis that humans had buried in their psyche. The natural telepathic abilities of my own people had been strengthened in the mix, and I knew that all I needed to do was to remove the iron collars from around one of our necks and they would be able to hear our thoughts, even if they were still halfway around the world.

I heard movement amongst the heap of ferns as Ameela woke. I had filled the collapsible mug with fresh water from the tortoise-shell I had fixed in the ground and carried it over to her.

She smiled and said, "Well that's the first night over. If our luck continues we might just see another one." She looked at the fire and added, "I don't want to push you, but we are running out of fuel."

I nodded. "I will do a little foraging and see what I can find nearby" I said. "In the meantime there are snake eggs in the embers and some cold bits of meat wrapped in leaves. Help yourself while I see what I can find."

"Be careful, Peterkin," She reminded me. "You are all I have out here until we are found. Just remember that Night Flower did not see death, but that's not to say we have nothing to worry about."

With those words hanging in the air I wandered down the slope and found a fallen tree which had easily removable dead branches. I bound the ends together with a vine and hauled them back to our camp. Several journeys up and down the slope and we had quite a pile of burnable fuel. Now we needed food and that might not be so easy. I made my way downhill again to see what I could find, leaving Ameela to feed the fire and burn some ferns to make plenty of smoke. She had managed to move around sitting on the belly armour plating that the tortoise had donated. Doing this she was able to gather more ferns for our bedding and anything else that came into her reach that might prove useful.

Then I saw something at the bottom of the slope, and at first I could not understand just what I was looking at. Something the size of a large boulder was slowly moving along. It was taller than me and was slowly ploughing through the brush with all the power of a human tank. I suddenly realised that it was a giant tortoise, the size of a small hut.

An idea presented itself, and I made my way towards it. I soon caught up with it and it ignored me until I got in front of it. Eyes larger than my fists stared uncomprehending at me, and it warned me away with a loud hiss of ill temper. The legs were almost thicker than my body and its shell was indeed just the size that would be big enough for two elves to shelter inside.

I sidestepped the great head and stepped to the side just behind the shoulder of the reptile, then thrust my hand against its armpit.

Immediately I was inside its tiny mind and had control of its nervous system. I climbed aboard and sat astride its neck. From here I had a slightly better view than on the ground. I was able to look down over the area where all the noise had been coming from last night, and could see that it was indeed a waterhole that was frequented by the various herds, day and night. My form of locomotion was slow, but it enabled me to infiltrate a herd of iguanodon without them noticing me. They were busy stripping a large fern of its greenery and the larger ones were bending the fronds down to the ground for the young to feast on the succulent upper growth. I singled out the largest of the group and eased the giant tortoise closer to the beast. As a tortoise, no matter how large, presented no threat, the dinosaurs totally ignored me and continued the strip the ferns and broke them down, where my ride helped itself to the juicy foliage. Without the iron torc around my neck I could have reached out to him and taken control, but I was handicapped and had to make a flesh contact to get into his mind, small though it was.

Whilst I had manoeuvred the giant tortoise closer to the herd of iguanodon I realised what an impossible task it would have been for me to clean out all the meat from inside this huge shell. Nevertheless its shell would make an ideal shelter for the two of us if I could only find a way to get it back. I wondered how long it would take if I left its carcass out on the plain for the carrion eaters to pick it clean and the insects to remove the rest.

I would soon have to make a decision as we ambled closer to the lead bull. So far it had remained dry, but when it rained we would have no shelter to speak of, so I reluctantly came to the conclusion that I would have to kill the animal. Then I thought that once his shell was empty I would be able to use the iguanodon to move it up the gentle slope to where we had made our campsite.

Sadly I entered the area of its mind that controlled the life functions and stopped the creature's heart. As the head dropped the full length of his neck upon the ground, I slid off into the small space between the iguanodon and the reptile. Before the creature could react I managed to lay my hands upon the soft skin of his leg and dominated his mind. I made several alterations to his way of thinking so that I became his young, to be protected at all costs. I made him stay still while I worked on what I could remove from the giant tortoise. I managed to cut into its throat and removed its tongue and a lot of its neck around the soft parts that would have been retracted into its shell. This I wrapped in the ferns and tied into a bundle so that my new servant would be able to haul it back.

He was quite nervous when he scented the blood, but I soon overrode his instincts and made him accept the parcels, which I began to tie across his back. Once I had climbed aboard and sat at the joint of neck and shoulders, he became more manageable. We had used these creatures as beasts of burden for many centuries due to their easy manageability. I made him stand up. Seeing the column of smoke from our fire, I headed towards Ameela.

My beast was thirty feet long from nose to tail and stood with its head sixteen feet above the ground, so Ameela would soon see what was paying her a visit.

As we got closer to the campsite I shouted out, "We have a helper, Ameela! Is everything OK with you?"

"How did you manage to get close enough to touch him?" she replied.

"I had some help there too, and once a few days have gone by we will have shelter too. I have meat that will last us for some time. I met a much larger cousin of the one you trapped yesterday and his shell is big enough to keep us both dry."

I slid off my mount and slipped off the vines, holding the bloody parcels of meat, and dragged them to the fire, placing them into the embers. I touched Ameela on her hand, entered her mind and showed her what I had done and what I planned to do.

"You feel that we could be here some time," she said. "It will take a while for the meat-eaters to strip the carcass down, and that will make that area dangerous. I promise you I will not let the fire go out."

I checked the stumps of her legs and was satisfied to see that the flesh was knitting together. I was sure that they were a little longer than when I had checked them last.

I looked up from my examination and said, "They are healing and growing, my queen, but it is too early to even guess how long it will take to grow back your feet."

"I am glad I am an elf, Peterkin, and can regrow my limbs in time, and not one of the many other creatures we share the parallel worlds with. This accident would have been final to a human or a dwarf," she replied in relief.

I fed the fire with some more of the wood I had gathered that morning and looked at what was left. It would only just make it through the night, so I turned to Ameela and said, "I will use our new friend to gather some more wood and carry it up here. Can you sort out the meat in the parcels while I am gone?"

She waved me away and began to undo the parcels while I re-joined my huge new friend. The iguanodon was where I had left him, feeding on the topmost branches it could find, and offered no protest as I remounted. From up here I could see and assess the situation as he stood on his hind legs. I was looking for dead trees whose branches could be hauled up the slope to where we had made our camp.

To the left of the trail I had used with the tortoise was the very thing that I was looking for. There was a large tree that had fallen in a storm, I supposed, and had dried out over the years. I urged my mount over to it and encouraged it to snap off the dead branches until there was a considerable pile. Now I insisted that the creature do something that was beyond his limited experience. I made him lean over, scoop up as many of the broken branches as he could hold against his chest and walk upright carrying them. He balanced the load using his tail and I used minimal coercion against his mind to achieve our needs. We did this journey over and over again until I was satisfied that we had enough wood to last for several days. I then encouraged him to regain his herd and return the next day to our shelter. He dropped down onto his front feet and I slid off the shoulders and onto the ground.

I watched him disappear down the slope and into the ferns and trees, avoiding the area around the dead tortoise. There was already plenty of action around the carcass as scavengers moved into the region, drawn by the smell of blood. This was not a place to be until the giant had been stripped clean.

We had a few hours before nightfall and I wanted to make sure that we were secure, so I gathered plenty of ferns to make a comfortable bed. I kept my spear very close to me and also gathered some of the supple vines that grew around the trees, winding them around my shoulders and chest. I drank several times from the tortoiseshell, which constantly filled with spring water. While I was in the vicinity of the large boulder that we camped against, I searched for dense, fist-sized rocks to make into hammers and anvils.

We sat that evening chewing on very tough and very old tortoise, but it filled the belly. There was plenty of it, so what we did not cook, we smoked to keep, avoiding the need to look for more food. There were plenty of the snake eggs left and they would last a few more days.

I had managed to use the reaching ability of our iguanodon to gather some fruit from the higher branches of a tree. The fruit was similar to a fig and some of them were quite sweet. We soon recognised the sour ones as the ones that were hard, and put these to one side. They would ripen in the sun and could be eaten another day. We baked the nuts in the centre of the fruit in the ashes of the fire to see if they could be made edible.

We were both so tired that we built up the fire and cuddled down in the bedding and I let Ameela sleep first and took first watch. I cradled her head in my lap and covered her with ferns to keep the cold night air at bay. I listened to the quarrelling sounds of the meat-eaters as they tore the giant tortoise apart and wondered if the shell would be empty by morning. I repeatedly added to the fire and kept it banked up and smoky so that the scent of the fire would deter the meat-eaters from wandering up the slope to the boulder we were camped against. The fact that there was a large store of meat would, I hoped, keep them occupied.

As the moon rose high above, I shook Ameela gently awake and kissed her forehead between her antennae. Then I entered her sleepy mind to say, "Time for me to sleep and you to keep watch over the fire. I love you and somehow we will get out of this fix, just as we did when I rescued you from the Tower of Absolom."

With that gentle mind touch, I burrowed into the ferns and went soundly to sleep to wait for the morning to dawn.

CHAPTER THIRTEEN

I awoke to the sounds of a crackling fire as Ameela fed another broken branch to the flames. She was toasting strips of tongue over the hot embers and had managed to crawl over to the upended tortoise shell and fill the collapsible mug with fresh water. She had buried this in the hot ashes and added a mixture of thinly-sliced meat, fruit and ground roasted nuts to make a soup. Whatever the collapsible mug had been made from it, seemed impervious to the fire. I wished that I had at my disposal all of the goodies that had been packed in our survival packs when we first dropped onto this world.

I sat up and groaned. Sore muscles took their toll as I pushed away the ferns.

"Good morning, High King," Ameela laughed. "How is the absolute ruler of the elfin commonwealth this morning?"

"He is missing his bed! If only we had Razzmandios here to look after us. He would come here and search for us if he could and woe betide anything that stood into his way."

"Well you will just have to make do with me, my lord. Now drink your soup and tell me what you have planned for today," she chuckled and handed me the hot drink she had made. I drank it down, bits and all, and followed it with strips of tortoise tongue and some of the fig-like fruit I had picked with the iguanodon's help. I had put a 'keep' in the lead bull's mind that should have kept him in the vicinity along with his herd.

They had probably moved into a defensive circle to deter the predators from transferring their interests from the dead giant tortoise to some of their own kind. Had I not had the iron torc welded shut around my neck, it would have been simplicity itself just to call him to me. I checked the fuel situation and found that we still had plenty to spare. I held Ameela's hand and quickly told her what I had in mind to do.

I finished my breakfast and stood up to scan down the slope to see if my new friend was in the vicinity. He was pulling down the tops of a tree to feed himself and the smaller members of his herd. I signalled to Ameela to be quiet and walked down the slope carrying our one and only spear, making sure he could see me. He stared at me and I could only imagine what was going through his mind as he recognised me as one of his young.

The lead bull dropped down on all fours and ambled up to me, and I cautiously approached him. Once he got my scent in his nostrils he became more positive and I was able to touch him to reinforce my mental control. The fact that the leader of the herd accepted me coerced the other members into allowing me to walk amongst them. I made the large bull stay and wait for me as I singled out a large female to mentally impress into my power. She snorted a warning which got a response from the bull that made her quiet and compliant. Once I could lay my hand upon her front leg, slipping into her mind was as simple as it could be, and once again I impressed into her mind that I was her chick and needed to be protected. I climbed onto her neck and shoulders and made her climb the gentle slope towards where Ameela was waiting.

She had packed up our meagre belongings, had made a bag out of her tunic to put them in and was ready to go. All I needed to do now was to somehow get her onto this great beast and we could explore the area together. I eased the female forward, made her lie full length on the ground and slid off. By scrabbling along on her knees Ameela managed to get to the iguanodon's neck and shoulders and swing her legs across so that both stumps were hanging down. I wound the vines I had collected last night around the female's neck so that Ameela had something to hold onto while the creature walked. Now that she was seated and in contact, she was quite easily able to control the beast with her mind.

I took the tunic that she had turned into a bag from her and tied it to the neck of my mount to keep it safe. She unfurled her wings and spread them out, so that they could help with the balancing problem she was having, without any feet to grip the dinosaur's neck. She smiled at me and a warm rush of love for this incredible woman filled my soul. Not once had she complained since the accident that had propelled us both onto the other side of the world. She was frightened, but would not give in to the fear that filled her mind. The one thing that kept our spirits up was that Night-Flower had not foreseen our deaths.

The problem we needed to resolve was how to retrieve the giant tortoise's shell from where the meat-eaters had left it. Once we had that cleaned out, we at least had a water-proof shelter that we could stuff with soft ferns and sleep inside with some protection from the weather. It did not take too long to find it. The night creatures had burrowed into the soft parts and had stripped it bare. There were a few large bones scattered about and that was all. There had been a lot of meat left inside that shell, and whatever headed up the food chain had fought each other over the rich pickings to be had. As soon as its belly had been filled, the top predator had moved on away from the competition to sleep it off in safety. I could only imagine what had gone on down here while we had kept the fire going.

I made the bull stay still while I investigated our prize and edged carefully up to the shell, which lay on its side. I poked the end of the spear into the inside and flushed out several small scavengers which had been picking the inside clean. It was still mucky inside and full of insects busy removing the last sticky bits. Apart from that, some improvements would help, and I threaded the supple vines I had collected through the front and back ends, twisting them together to make them stronger. I wove the ends into a loop and went back to my mount. Once I could touch him I began to bend him to my will and made him put his head and neck through the loop. The spring that supplied us with fresh water emptied into a pool that was the local watering hole. I had decided to use this as a cleansing place for the insect-riddled shell, and the iguanodons were going to become my haulage creatures.

I shouted across to Ameela, "I'm going to get him to pull the shell into the pond to clean it. Make your beast useful by making her push the shell while this one drags it into the water."

She nodded and lined up her beast behind the shell as I got my iguanodon to pull the shell into the pool. I became him and used his muscles as if he was a puppet. He was immensely strong and once we got moving, the shell was easy to manoeuvre. We crushed down the reeds at the edge of the pond and waded into the depths, dragging the shell behind us.

The shell proved to be a lot lighter than I had imagined; in fact it almost floated. We allowed the sun to get quite high in the sky before we dragged the empty shell out of the pool and onto dry land. I felt a momentary pang of sorrow for the previous inhabitant, but finding an empty shell somewhere would have been an impossible task.

By using the two 'pressed' iguanodons it did not take long to manoeuvre our new shelter into a settled position. The fire was still piled high with hot embers, so we soon coaxed it back to life. After several trips to the pool I had managed to obtain a good bundle of reeds for Ameela to weave into baskets. The roots of the reeds made good eating once roasted in the embers and we still had a quantity of the tortoise meat we had smoked. I gathered armfuls of ferns to make our bedding and made a smoky fire inside the shell to drive out the remaining insects.

Towards evening I dragged the fire out of the shell and swept what remained into our main fire, then checked the stock of branches, which I had added to. We had set the two iguanodon to blockade the entrance to our new home and kept the herd nearby. For the first time in what seemed ages, we would sleep together without needing to keep watch.

Barathon and Petronius immersed themselves in rapport with the Spellbinder's composite mind and searched for their parents with no result. Vinr had taken her ship into a close drift over the land that had been torched by the Breath of the Sun to see what John had unleashed. For miles in every direction the very ground and rocks had turned into gas, leaving a molten trail across the lands. The air had become super-heated and had killed every air-breathing creature in the vicinity for fifty miles around the path of the 'Breath'. Fires still burned, raging through what had been turned into tinder dry kindling by the intense heat. The rush of hot air fountaining into the atmosphere had drawn in the cold air from the mountains and seas, causing thunderstorms to empty cascading rain onto the fires. Smoke and steam whirled and twisted over a dead land. What the heat had not killed, the radioactivity of the sun had poisoned. Lakes had boiled and all vegetable life was turned to charcoal in the path of the beam.

Nuzac and Vinr stared at the desolation in horror, passing the information back to John Smith in the goblin ship and the elves in the original Spellbinder.

"I have learnt a terrible thing this day, Chisbolt, and that is the fact that if we have to, we can sterilise this world and totally destroy the Collective," John said to his goblin friend.

Chisbolt Hungry-jaw just stood, staring back at him with his green face pale and drawn. "That could only come from a human!" he replied. "What you are saying is unthinkable. We cannot destroy a world!"

"That is not our decision to make, old friend," he replied. "That thing down there wrested control from me at the exit end of the 'Breath' and caused all that damage that you can see through Vinr's sensors. If it can do that, how long will it be before it opens a Rift on our home-worlds and seeds them? The only good thing that has come out of this is that the shock of incinerating part of its static forms seems to have put it into a catatonic state. What happens when it wakes up?"

"We need Peterkin. This is far too much responsibility to carry on our shoulders. He is somewhere on this world with an injured Ameela to look after. We have to find them," Chisbolt said. "Surviving on that dinosaur-dominated world would be difficult enough without losing your feet and being unable to stand."

"They could be anywhere, down there, old friend, anywhere at all. All we have to go on in our favour is that No'tt-mjool says that she is sure they are both still alive and that she cannot 'see' a future that does not include them. She says she would be aware of a space in the future where they occupy. More than that, she will not say."

Barathon broke into their conversation and broadcast to each mind, "We will start searching this world by the continents that have formed. We will search Europe and Asia where the beam has not touched, above the equator. Vinr will take below the equator and search Africa, India and Australia. I want you, John and Chisbolt to concentrate on the continent of the Americas. Meanwhile I have sent a mental summons to every Spellbinder and its crew to get here as soon as they can. When they do I will allocate them to become your wingmen and broaden the search. Look for the smoke from a fire, as that will be a sure sign from my father. He will do this knowing that it will be something that we would look for. There will be many false alarms, because we know that the raptors of this world have discovered how to use and make fire. Nevertheless, check each column of smoke and overlook nothing."

The three Spellbinders broke formation and began their almost impossible tasks, making a start across the dinosaur world, keeping a mental watch just in case there was some telepathic thread to follow. As the days wore on without a result, more and more Spellbinders joined in the search, including Mia, who drove the search patterns relentlessly searching for her mother and father. Still, No'tt-mjool insisted that both elves were still alive and there was no empty space in the future. Linked to her mind, her partner, Sam Pitts continually scanned the many different threads that led to the future, looking for some clue as to where his friend might be.

As the days passed, I became aware that the area where we had landed was rapidly being depleted of fuel and food. The herd of iguanodon had stripped every vestige of greenery from the surrounding countryside and desperately needed to find fresh pastures. Apart from that, the heaps of dung they deposited had become unpleasant to live with, so I decided to hitch up our shell home to the large bull and move to another part of this world.

Ameela had by now grown new ankles and her feet had

begun to form. We had hammered away at the iron torcs and had managed to flatten them a little, but we were a long way from getting free of them. I had managed to touch all the members of the herd over the days we had spent in their company and had instilled a desire to protect us in all of them. They had got used to our fire and no longer reacted when wisps of smoke happened to come their way.

Reluctantly I put the fire out and harnessed the bull iguanodon to the shell, but I did keep a glowing coal in a nest of damp leaves, surrounded by slow burning materials. If it did not keep alight I still had my fire-making materials packed away in the shell. We had made baskets from the reeds and had filled them with anything useful such as the stone tools we had made. Ameela's years marooned on the top of the Tower of Absolom had made her very self-reliant on what she could manufacture herself.

I induced the big male to follow the herd as they flattened a pathway through the jungle led by Ameela, who was seated on her mount's shoulders. I followed behind, making sure that the harness remained intact and our 'temporary' home stayed attached. I had spent a long time twisting the supple vines together to make them strong, so I was reasonably confident that all would remain well.

I had taken flight several times to have a good look around and had found a steady rise in the distance that looked as if it would break into a good-sized set of hills at the base of a large plateau. Hopefully there might be a cliff that we could anchor our shell against to give us some protection. I definitely wanted to stay away from the huge black trees, which were now growing vigorously toward the clouds and sprouting out of the emergent layer above the canopy. Several times I was sure I could see smoke lifting into the sky, quite some distance away. It was frustrating not to be able to fly closer, but the air was anything but empty and the pterodactyls constantly hunted creatures the same size as me.

We had some good fortune as the herd walked through a nesting site and I was able to collect baskets of eggs and store them in the shell. I managed to wring the necks of a number of hatchlings and added them to the store of food, along with fruit that we managed to pick from the trees as we passed.

The position where we were making our new home was well sheltered from a frontal attack by being on a natural platform raised up from the jungle floor. It had taken some effort to push the giant tortoise shell into position using an iguanodon each, but we had managed it. I made the lead bull shove the tortoise shell against the side of the hill we had been marching to and I released them to forage amongst the foliage, while I collected some dead wood. To my delight my coal was still alight and glowing, so with some steady blowing I brought the fire back to life. I managed to find a large flat stone and banked a small fire onto this, just outside the giant tortoise shell, making very sure that it was safe and secure. Once again we had water from a spring that oozed out of the cliff-face and we directed it into the small tortoise shell. I filled the collapsible mug and we both drank deeply.

"Have you noticed, Ameela, there are scorch marks on the ground around here caused by fire?" I said. "I will go and collect more firewood to make sure that we do not run out. If we build a decent size fire we might just get some company."

"Be careful, Peterkin. We are new to this area so stay close to our herd and take no chances," Ameela pleaded as she fed another piece of dead wood into the fire.

I looked up to the sky and judged that the sun would still be up for another few hours. I made my way down the slope of the hill and climbed aboard my iguanodon. I had spotted an overturned tree on the way up and had marked it in my mind as a good source of firewood. It did not take very long to get to the broken branches and I used the big male as a bulldozer by ripping off the deadwood from the main stem. Once a sizable amount had been collected, I tied it into a large bundle and hauled it back up the slope to our new campsite. The animals on this world had no fear of us, as we did not conform to any dangerous life form, and killing them was easy with a spear.

I had collected another large snake from under the dead tree and had gutted it where I killed it. Once again I found where the eggs had been buried and filled a basket with them. They were quite fresh and I opened one up to make sure and drank the contents.

My mount and I made our way back to the camp, and once I had coerced the iguanodon to push our wood into a manageable pile I released my control over it so that it could go back to the herd and keep them in the vicinity. So far we had not been too troubled by carnosaurs, but there were always some following the herd. A group of allosaurus had shadowed us for the best part of the day and I felt that come night-time they were sure to pick off one of the weakest of the herd. We would not be sleeping at the same time tonight, and whoever was awake would need to keep the fire alight and smoky as it was the scent of smoke that kept the meat-eaters away.

Ameela took the first watch. There was a steady drizzle pouring down outside the shell, so it was imperative that she keep the fire burning. I had constructed a rude shelter over the fire to stop the rain from extinguishing the flames and we had an overhang that helped to keep the majority of the weather at bay. The moon was obscured by heavy clouds, so on the approach to our camp it was almost impossible to see more than a few feet down the slope. It was a hunter's night, for anything that had a good sense of smell.

The pack of allosaurus had moved through the night, guided by their superb sense of smell to the outskirts of the herd. Three of the pack remained hidden while two of the junior killers edged around the herd until they were opposite the three that lay in wait. Once they were there they urinated over the bushes, letting the constant drizzle wash the heavy scent towards the herd. The strong scent of the carnosaurs' urine made the senior members of the herd uneasy, and they grouped towards the threat to meet it head on. The ones at the back turned to face whatever was coming towards them and turned their backs upon the three allosaurus waiting for this to happen. They charged through the gaps and with a number of swift bites and a disembowelling strike, they killed several of the younger ones and scattered the herd.

Ameela shook me awake and said, "The herd has been attacked. I doubt that they will regroup anywhere near to where we are in the morning. I am too tired to keep awake any longer, so my love, you are on fire watch!"

I kissed her forehead between her antennae, pulled the ferns over her to keep warm and said, "Maybe the sun will break through in the morning. It would be nice to be warm again. What I would give for a hunk of gnome-backed bread and a slab of cheese!"

With that I wriggled out into the cold, fire-lit darkness and threw some more logs upon the fire. The rain had eased off, but the darkness remained impenetrable to my senses. What I could not see I could imagine, and I gripped my spear in foolish defiance. The two of us had been incredibly lucky so far and the iguanodon herd had kept us relatively safe, but if the allosaurus had indeed scattered the herd, then retrieving any of the 'pressed' dinosaurs would be very uncertain.

After what seemed a terribly long time the first rosy fingers of dawn began to claim the sky and it began to lighten. The clouds had thinned out and most of the rain-bearing ones had dissipated. I fed the fire with more branches and added some green fronds to make plenty of smoke to advertise our presence to the local carnosaurs, hoping they might move off.

The smoke also helped to drive off the clouds of flies that wanted to feast on our unprotected skin. Our tunics were filthy and needed washing out, and my boots were falling apart. We were steadily regressing to our beginnings, to a more simple existence, and would soon have to live naked, once the only cloth we had disintegrated through excessive wear and tear. Keeping warm on cold wet nights meant burrowing underneath ferns which we collected and dried out. We would shake them out over the smoke to dislodge the insects and other life that stubbornly clung on.

As the giant tortoise shell dried out and the last vestiges of its occupant were cleaned out by ants it became a more comfortable and clean place to shelter inside. Nevertheless I vigorously brushed it out each morning and left a smouldering heap of ferns inside to deter any visitors while we breakfasted on whatever I had managed to find during the day.

I let the sun rise in the sky and send some penetrating warmth before I woke Ameela and sorted through what food we had accumulated. We still had some smoked hatchlings which I had collected from the nesting site the iguanodon had disturbed. They were stringy, but the hind legs were quite plump and there was meat to be found if you were hungry enough. There were plenty of snake eggs in the basket, so I rolled six of them into the embers of the fire wrapped in broad leaves to stop the shells from burning. I heaped the ashes over the top of them and went inside our shelter to wake Ameela.

She was awake and sitting up in the middle of a heap of ferns, vigorously scratching where something had bitten her. Her new feet were peeping out from the greenery and soon she would be able to walk on them. At the moment they were all complete, but the size of a child's and far too small to risk standing on them. We both knew that the bones would not be strong enough to take her weight as yet. Judging by the rate of growth, it would only take a few more days before she would be able to start learning to walk again.

I helped her outside and tossed some of the fire onto the old bedding to set it alight and smoke out the night-time occupants. We sat together and ate what I had buried in the embers of the fire, drinking from my collapsible mug.

Ameela grabbed hold of my arm and spoke into my mind, "We have visitors!"

I turned, slowly stood up and laid my spear on the ground. Then I made the sign of empty hands to a group of velociraptors which were walking cautiously towards us. All of them wore rooted seeds at the backs of their heads. They all had leather bags strapped across their shoulders and belts around their waists carrying tools on loops. Each of them carried a flint-topped spear in one hand, much heavier than mine, and they too laid them on the ground.

They had seen the smoke and found us. Now I needed to get one of the raptors to allow me to touch one of them so that I could converse telepathically.

CHAPTER FOURTEEN

I motioned to the fire and to our basket of cooked eggs for them to share our food. One of them reached into the bag on his shoulders and produced several large strips of meat that had to have come from one of the iguanodon killed by the allosaurus during the night.

These velociraptors were much larger than the ones we had been accustomed to on the other side of the world and on our own. They had the same golden eyes, and they too had feathers growing along their arms with a set of finer ones climbing up their necks until they became a coloured crest. They too had three-fingered hands with opposable thumbs. We had improved the thumb by genetic manipulation and any velociraptor that hatched without a thumb was immediately killed. I suspected that this practise was adhered to on this world, before the Collective had enslaved them all. They had the same type of disembowelling talon on their feet. Evolution on this continent had also produced a much heavier-set velociraptor; whether that meant that other dinosaurs had become a lot bigger here would soon become apparent.

The raptor carrying the meat skewered them onto a fire-blackened stick and placed it over the flames to cook. The group settled by our fire and showed no fear of us or animosity once they had recognised Ameela and me as the elves that their cousins had met on the other side of the world.

What the Collective had learnt about us had been shared with every velociraptor on this planet.

The leader of the group walked around the fire and stared at our shelter with some interest before she motioned me to sit, while she squatted by the side of me. She held out her clawed hand to mine and I gripped my fingers around her wrist. Instantly I was inside her mind and was able to make a telepathic link.

She spoke first. "You are the newcomers to our world" she said. The Voice that Tells has told us much about you. Why is the Voice that Tells silent, and why are you here?"

I gently gave her as much information as I thought she could understand about my people and the parallel worlds. Most of all I reassured her that we meant no harm to her people, and I tried to explain about the alien life-form that had reached this world.

I asked her "Can you remove this circle around my neck to allow me to talk with you more easily?"

She stared at the iron torc that was welded shut, and gripped it tightly with her powerful hands. I explained what I thought would make it snap and she began to bend it back and forth until metal fatigue began to make the material crack. At last the iron split open and the circle of metal was removed from around my neck. My mind was free. I asked if she could do the same for Ameela and she did so, snapping the torc using the same method. I sent my mind out and across the world and found that to my surprise it was mentally silent from the alien presence. We both made contact with our extended family scattered across the heavens and the hundreds of Spellbinders, to say that we were both alive and well.

I found John Smith and saw the awful destruction that Breath of the Sun had wrought across the European continent. I realised what it meant. Broadening the field of contact, I then told them all to do nothing more than stay in position, send my ship to where we were and keep out of sight. I added a clear command to destroy any kind of seed-case that might come shooting into the sky. That I added only as a precaution, as the real threat would be the Collective's seeds spreading through the multiverse via the Rifts.

When I returned to the present, I was aware that the leader of the troop was staring at me with some concern. We two elves had switched off our bodies and frozen where we sat while our minds had dealt with the searchers' myriad questions. Ameela was still 'talking' to her children and grandchildren and reassuring them that she would not still need the legs and feet which they had stored in a stasis chamber.

"Thank you, leader of your people, for removing the shield" I said. "I had hoped that you would see the smoke and find us. There is much that we need to know about what you call 'The Voice that Tells' and how it has changed your lives."

"Life is much better now," the raptor replied. "We now have the gift of speaking in our heads. All who carry the seed do so with pride. The great eaters can be controlled and are no longer a threat. We feed them to the trees, along with the giant long-necks, and take our pick of what we need. The smaller carrion eaters and hunters we cull from time to time; they are a necessity to the ecology. This the Voice has shown us."

I thought about what the big female said and answered, "But what free will do you possess? We are not ruled and controlled as you are. This idea is not something that we can permit to spread."

She stared at me and raised her crest before replying, "This was so at the beginning when the Voice first made contact with us. It took a while and then things changed. We now have purpose in our lives where before there was none, except to survive. There is time now to think and plan, where once just to stay alive was enough. I can speak to any other raptor on this world without even seeing them. We are all joined by our minds, just like you, whereas before the Voice came, we lived in darkness and ignorance of each other."

I sat and pondered what she had told me, thinking inwards to speak with the long-dead kings of the Spellbinder. The original High King, Freyr, was the first to speak.

"Peterkin, ask yourself, would you plunge this world back into anarchy? If you used the Breath of the Sun to burn each and every tree, would these people still remain telepaths? It seems to me that only those who carry the seeds have this power."

Auberon, the High King on Earth, made another point. "These people are the responsibility of the High King now that they have been discovered. You, Peterkin, have spread the civilization of the elfin kingdom over many worlds as they have been discovered and settled by all the sentient races under your rule. It was your decision to clone the Spellbinder into a fleet of ships and pass them out to everyone. It was the raptors that discovered this world in a different parallel universe. This could not be foreseen. The problem however will not go away, and when the alien creature re-emerges you will need something to offer it. Not only that, you will need to be able to control it, or destroy it."

The other minds agreed that a less destructive way must be found to solve the problem. Scorching this world into a ball of fire could not be envisaged, except possibly as a last resort. I had seen the effect that John's loss of control had had on the other side of this world and was fully aware of what could be done. It would take centuries for the land to recover from being turned into a molten pile of slag. The people we had met had been swallowed up in the fiery 'Breath' and had died along with every other living thing in that area. Now that the mind of the Collective had shut down, the restrictions placed by it on the growth of the trees had been lifted. They had all burst into sight and attained their maximum growth. Now they stood two miles high and half a mile across the root system at the base. They were no longer hidden from view. There must now be a multitude of Spellbinders in orbit around this planet, all equipped with the knowledge of how to use the Breath of the Sun. I gave orders to seek out each and every one of the 'Trees' and stay nearby, but not to do anything until I gave the order to do so.

A great dark shadow materialised over the campsite and I realised that my sons had arrived. I spoke directly to the mind of the leader. "Do not be alarmed. The shadow over us is my means of travelling across this world and to others. We shall have to leave you for a short time while we re-enter the ship and refresh ourselves. We will come back, I promise."

Above us the Spellbinder had sprouted legs and touched down, so that it was fixed to where we were camped. Ameela had two things on her mind, a refreshing shower and a clean set of clothes. The problem was that her new feet were still far too small to be walked on, but that difficulty was soon sorted when my two granddaughters, Brianna and Kellynn, appeared from the nearest leg and picked her up with their telekinetic ability. They loaded her back onto the Spellbinder and disappeared with her.

I turned to the raptor and said, "Please help yourself to whatever food we have gathered as I have sufficient stored on board my ship". I placed my hand upon her chest and repeated, "I will come back and see you. There is still much we need to talk about".

I walked over to where the leg of the Spellbinder was fixed to the ground and was accepted into the structure and propelled upwards to the control chamber. When I stepped out, my son Barathon met me and recoiled as my scent hit his nostrils.

"Ye gods Father, you stink to high heaven! Spellbinder, give him a shower where he stands!"

Immediately I was encased in four walls and sluiced down with warm soapy water which removed the accumulated filth that clung to my body and hair. I dropped my soiled tunic and shorts to the floor and spread my wings. This was to remove all traces of blood and mud from the tiny feathers that lined the membranes and folds of skin that stretched from my bony second fingers. These arms were much wider than the two that were used normally, and opened like a bat's. When not in use, they folded several times until they slipped into a receptacle at the back. The humans had always been amazed at how our wings could extend outwards so far and tuck away so neatly.

Once I was clean, the walls retracted into the floor along with the muck that had been sluiced from me. My sons were nearby and were ready with a fresh tunic and pants. To my surprise Ameela was also washed and freshly clothed, but standing on her own two feet.

"Our grandchildren have all donated some of their life-force to speed up the healing process and regrow what was needed. I am as good as new," she smiled and leaned forward to kiss me.

"It is really great to have you back, father," Barathon said and gave me a hug. "No'tt-mjool gave us hope that you were still alive, as she was sure that the future had no empty space in it where you and mother should be. We would have searched for you for a thousand years as long as we had that hope!"

"Thank you son," I replied. "We both knew that you would not abandon us while there was hope, but I have to tell you that mother and I must go back down to the velociraptors that found us and released us from the iron torcs."

"Why, when you are safe and sound on board the Spellbinder, would the two of you return? Surely all we have to do is to burn all traces of the Trees from this planet and leave," retorted Polonius, shaking his head in disbelief.

"My sons and grandchildren, listen to what I have to say. This is an almost immortal sentient life-form which has altered the eco-system to suit not only itself but the intelligent raptors that serve it. Serve may be too strong a description of the relationship. I would call it more a symbiosis than just servitude. I need to know more about this creature, because when it re-awakens I feel there may be a lot more to make decisions about than now. We have demonstrated our power and by now each two-mile high Tree will have made itself conspicuous and been logged by a Spellbinder."

Firovel answered, "Then this is the time to destroy them all! While that thing 'sleeps' it is defenceless, so I say that we destroy it now. Burn every giant growth into ash."

"Have you fallen so far from the tree that you can only think like a Dokka'lfar?" I replied angrily, and with some despair. "These people are the responsibility of the High King. Even this alien being becomes part of that mantle if possible. I give what thanks I have that you are far from the post of leader of the elfin community and the commonwealth that I have built up. My remaining years will still be devoted to that ideal and I can only hope that when it is time for me to depart that you or one of the others is ready to pick up this mantle."

I felt the stir from within all the long-dead Kings that I carried in my mind. Their shock and horror echoed through my mind as they considered my situation and the line of succession that spiralled into an uncertain future. I had allowed a genetic twist into the elfin bloodlines by allowing the insertion of human genes, to allow the gift of telekinesis to emerge. Even the tainted bloodline of Molock himself dwelt beneath the surface of my people. It was diluted for sure, but every so often it emerged in attitudes that were not those of the Ljo'sa'lfar, and it bothered me. I had taken the crown through an incredible act of violence from the mad King Waldwick, who had murdered my father and his brother to get it. I too was tainted by having the ability to kill handed down to me by 'royal' lineage, but I had controlled that ability and still had it under tight control.

I considered the facts I had at my disposal. This alien creature had lived an incredibly long time, spreading its seeds through time and space operating by instinct alone. Now, because it had chanced upon a world inhabited by intelligent beings, it too had assumed the mantle of sapience. It had adapted rapidly to what it had found and absorbed. At the beginning of its ruthless domination the raptors had thoughtlessly served. As time went by a richer interdependence had altered the whole mind-set. It had reached out to control the rift manipulated by my friend John Smith and had paid a terrible price for it. Yet it had managed to take control away from a Halfling that was used to that power. The question begged to be asked - what could it do in the future?

I turned to Brianna and Kellynn and asked, "Could you take a portion of Elf-stone and modify the giant tortoise shell to be more habitable? Your grandmother and I will be living inside it for a while, so we will need toilet facilities, storage cabinets and a comfortable bed. We are going to live with the velociraptors and understand more about what has gone on this side of the world while we were concentrating on the one Tree in Europe. When the Collective re-awakens I want to be found living within the raptors' protection and not seen as an enemy."

"I was too hasty, grandfather," Firovel said with heartfelt

contrition. "It seemed to be the logical thing to do to rid us of this menace."

"Grandson, you have not thought the problem through far enough. The seed-case that fell upon this world had travelled the star-lanes for maybe millions of years and when it arrived here it immediately took control. Within a short time the Collective merged into the eco-system and was successfully manipulating it to serve its own uses. If it could sleep for that length of time in deep space, how long do you think it could spend in suspended animation here? If you removed every Tree from this world, you would then need to hunt down every velociraptor that carried a seed and burn it. Think on, Firovel, beyond that point. What of the seeds that lay buried in the ground, waiting maybe hundreds of thousands of years before germinating and spreading their influence all over again when this has been forgotten? Time is on the side of this organism. No, my children! There is far more to think about than destroying the Trees that we can find and see."

I ate several buttered bread rolls with cheese and drank a large mug of gnomish cold beer before I decided to return to the surface and reacquaint myself with the raptors at the campsite. First I packed a survival pack that carried tools, dried foods, cord and bottle-bags to store water in.

"I have to go back, Ameela. Are you coming with me?" I asked.

Ameela shook her head in disbelief at such a suggestion and replied, "Do not think for one moment, Peterkin, that you will go down there alone. Where you go, I go and that's the end of it! I have not packed this rucksack to sit about in here."

My four grandchildren answered with one common voice, "We will go too. You may need our abilities and we are sure that Barathon and Polonius can handle the Spellbinder without us under their feet. Besides which, our control of the Elf-stone can make things a lot more comfortable when we get to where the raptors live."

I smiled to myself in satisfaction and said, "Make your way to the exit and back to the campsite. We will need a harness for the iguanodon to pull the tortoise shell behind it, far better than the twisted vines that I used. He should be somewhere nearby with his herd so call him and he will come. My imprint will be on his mind."

Before I left, I contacted John Smith and asked him to relay to me just what had happened when he had lost control of the Breath of the Sun. He was definite in his reasoning that he had control wrested away from him just as he opened the rift to what was supposed to be a narrow beam. The Collective had opened the Rift wide, destroying the static form at that place and sending itself into a catatonic state through the shock of its destruction. John had managed to close the Rift adjacent to the sun, but not before the 'Breath' swung through the shelter that my grandchildren had built. It was this cross-sectional twist that intersected the Rift back to the Spellbinder that had sent Ameela and me halfway across the planet. Ameela had just got her feet onto the Spellbinder when the Rift shifted, slicing them off.

The important thing to remember was that this organism had seized hold of the Rift and altered the size of it. What it had clumsily done before, it might well learn to become adept at controlling, and then the multiverse would be open to its whims. I had to stop this from happening, no matter what.

"Thank you John," I said, "for all that you have done for me. If I should fail at containing this alien life-form, this world must die. It must be sterilised completely and left lifeless. That includes everyone who is down there at the time if I give the order."

"High King! I cannot condemn this teeming world to a full

onslaught of the Breath of the Sun. What you ask is beyond my moral capability to perform. I could not live with the responsibility of sterilising a world. Please, Peterkin, do not lay that burden upon me!"

I reached into his mind and did what had to be done to take away all responsibility from the actions that I hoped would not be necessary. I planted the command that would see the awful deed done if I released the trigger. If I needed him, he would be there and my will would be done. The responsibility would be mine and mine alone, as befits a High King.

I kissed both of my sons and walked across the Spellbinder's floor to the leg that would take me down to the campsite where the raptors waited for me.

As I dropped to the ground I felt the mind of my daughter, Mia, enter mine and say, "Father, I can see what you have in mind if forced to do. What will the commonwealth do without your guidance? You know that neither Barathon nor Polonius are ready for that mantle of accountability."

"You are my dearly beloved daughter," I answered. "You would make a great High Queen! If I have to leave things in your hands you will find that you will get help from all the long dead Kings. You will grow used to their advice dictated from the Spellbinder. I too will be there to counsel you, as a copy of my mind. Now dry your tears and do not fear for the worst. I may yet find a way to contain this threat. Do you think that I would not try everything at my disposal before unleashing this final solution? One more thing. Look after my old friend John Smith, if the worst comes to fruition. He will need you. Now I must go. Never forget that I love you, my daughter. Take care."

I walked out of the embrace of my Spellbinder and saw that my grandchildren had been active with the giant tortoise shell. Anchor points had been 'grown' from the shell above where the shoulders would have been and the straps from the ship had been attached to these and harnessed to the iguanodon.

I entered the shell and looked around at the changes. There were two beds set against the walls, with a drawer under each bed. These had been filled with all manner of items that my grandchildren had deemed useful. There was enough space between the beds to be able to walk through. Water tanks were bedded into the sloping walls and would be filled when it rained by diverting the flow from the natural slope of the top of the shell into gullies. This was incredible luxury.

I dumped my rucksack inside and approached the leader of the raptors. I held out my hands in welcome and said, "May we now return to your settlement? There is much that I would learn, for when the Voice that Tells awakens, as I am sure it will, I will speak with it."

She spoke rapidly to her companions to lead the way and I felt her mind contact mine as she asked, "What will you do once you have reached our settlement? I am Vinr-tat, leader of many villages and responsible for my people's safety. I would know your name and title also?"

I replied, "I am called Peterkin and I am responsible to all who live within my Commonwealth. There are many different species of sentient beings that live beneath my patronage and their wellbeing is my obligation to maintain. My title is High King and I have the power of life or death over all who live within my realm."

"You have an awesome power at your command," Vinr-tat replied. "I have seen it through the eyes of those who were not destroyed by the power of the sun. It is a terrible thing to see!"

For a few moments I stood looking at this creature that could quite easily tear me apart, before continuing to walk beside her.

"I do not wish to do this again" I answered. "It was an accident that will not be repeated. The Voice that Tells interfered in what we felt forced into doing. Now another solution must be found if it can be accomplished. But first I must learn all that I can from you about what you have achieved living in this new way and what the Voice that Tells does for you in return for your servitude."

I 'called' over one of the herd that was travelling with us and made it lie down so that the two of us could climb aboard. We settled into where the neck joined the shoulders and let the beast plod steadily along, following the lead male, pulling our temporary shelter. As we travelled along I extracted as much relevant information from the raptor's mind as I needed about the Collective and how these people lived under its rule.

CHAPTER FIFTEEN

It took a week to make our way to where the velociraptors had their settlement. Meanwhile we used the giant tortoise shell as a refuge from the rainstorms and a safe place to sleep. The water catchments worked well and kept our tanks well filled. My grandchildren slept outside and took it in turns to sleep shifts and keep watch, although our new large friends also did the same and kept the fire going through the night.

As the pack of allosaurus continued to follow the herd of iguanodon, Firovel and Cethafin decided to remove them from the caravan. They waited behind one late afternoon and sure enough some distance from the back of the herd, five allosaurus were stealthily edging towards one of the young iguanodon to take him.

They could quite easily have killed them all, by just reaching out and stopping their hearts, but instead they conjured a forest fire between the back of the herd and the stalking beasts. They filled their tiny minds with panic and smoke, causing them to break off the kill and stampede through the underbrush away from the herd that was making towards the settlement.

We eventually came to a wide river which had curved to produce an ox-bow lake in its wandering down to the sea. In this protected haven the raptors had built a stockade across the edges of the bends, blending the upright stakes into the natural trees and weaving vines between living and dead wood. The ground had been cleared in front of the enclosure to allow the raptors inside a clear view of what might approach them. I marvelled at what they had accomplished under the direction of the alien invader in such a short time. From the memories tucked inside Vinr-tat's mind I could see that they had settled here in this ox-bow for some generations, but had not thought to improve the defences, which would have proved useless against the huge dinosaurs; they would easily have ploughed through them.

The mental control that the Collective had transferred into these people meant they had thinned the herds of giant sauropods down by 'feeding' them to the local 'Tree' along with the larger predators such as the T Rex. Now, the fence of the stockade deterred the medium-sized beasts from entering and even kept those that they wished to keep inside ready for slaughter. For the first time in generations these intelligent velociraptors had a place of safety to retreat to and sleep unmenaced. If I destroyed the Collective, would the mental powers of these people vanish and propel them back into a fight for existence?

Ameela and I walked into the settlement, to be greeted by a crowd of curious raptors of all ages. Not all of them carried the Star-Seeds, and it was easily apparent to us what a difference the implanting of a seed made to each affected raptor. It was then the obvious fact struck me that they shared a common consciousness, and in doing so had increased their intelligence. Within a few months they had increased their rate of evolution by many generations. If I had to destroy these people to keep my own confederation safe from the Collective's domination, the burden of doing so would break my mind. I had inherited my ability to kill from my 'kingly' line, but to order death on this scale would send me mad. To ensure that this alien life-form could be contained and its menace removed, I would have to consign this abundant world to the flames of the sun, leaving nothing alive anywhere. If I had to trip that trigger implanted in my old friend's mind, I would stay on this world and die with it. John would carry out my orders, because he could not disobey them, but whether he could live with himself afterwards, I just could not know.

My thoughts had leaked from my mind and I was aware of Ameela staring at me in horror. "Peterkin, no! Not that, my dearest love, not that! The death of a world to save our people! No-one should have to hold that burden alone. If there is no alternative, then I will not leave your side. There has to be another way! There has to," and she held tightly to my hand so that not a stray thought escaped.

"I have told Mia that should this unthinkable thing be necessary then she must become the first High Queen, as neither of our sons is ready for that kind of responsibility, or our grandchildren" I replied. "Oh, Ameela my love, I have tormented my soul with that lesser problem, but can see no other way to resolve it. There is one thing that still remains in my mind and it was something that No'tt-mjool said, something I still cannot make any sense of. She said she could not see a space in the fabric of space-time concerning us at all, no matter how far she looked into the future. That does not make any sense at all."

"She is a strange troll, is Night Flower," Ameela agreed, "But she has never been wrong with that sense of hers. Remember what the spirit of the dwarf Cailleach the prophetess saw in you - a strange destiny that she would not explain. She said that you had much to do and there would be more than one struggle and many paths to take."

I shuddered as I remembered when Hildegard had brought Cailleach from the realms of the dead for that long-dead seeress to speak to me. There was the way that she regarded me, which affected my reasoning. She had cut short her thoughts from me, but there was left just fleetingly, a feeling of awe regarding my destiny, and then it was gone. It had taken some centuries, but eventually I had reclaimed my grandchildren from the mind-bending that Eloen had subjected them to. They carried the genetic flaw however of the heritage of Molock, who had spawned the Dokka'lfar branch of the elfin race, spreading his mutation and forcing the Ljo'sa'lfar to flee from their ancestral home. In the end I had destroyed them all and had formed the 'Great Commonwealth', a mixture of many different sentient beings under my leadership. I had become High King of all the many races under my protection. The humans called it a benevolent dictatorship, and judging by their past experiences they were quite happy to live under my monocratic rule.

In a telepathic society, murder, warfare and any act of violence could not be entertained. Eloen's capacity for these attributes would not be repeated as long as I lived. Soon however, the time would come when my span would become finite and I would have to leave all that I had built in the hands of another. All I could do was to leave things as well-ordered as I could and the problem of the Collective would have to be resolved by me and me alone.

Sam Pitts interrupted my morose thoughts with uneasy news. "Long Shadow, I have news from Night Flower" he said. "She sees the awakening of the Collective in the near future and advises you to be ready."

I stared up to the clouds far above and asked, "Where are you, old friend?"

"Our Spellbinder is tethered above the Tree that these people serve. Every Tree has been accounted for and has a Spellbinder within range. We can hit every single one with the Breath of the Sun at your command."

"Thank you Sam, but it is far more complicated than just that. Do nothing without my instruction, but keep in a state of readiness," I replied and again reached for Ameela's hand.

"Ameela, the Collective wakens soon. We must be ready to do whatever is necessary to keep our people safe. You and the grandchildren should return to my Spellbinder commanded by our sons. There you will be safe no matter what I decide."

"Whatever you decide to do, I will not leave your side!" she declared with tears running down her face. "Peterkin, you are the breath of life to me and if it is to be stilled along with yours, then so be it. Send the grandchildren back by all means, but be sure that I will not be going with them. How could I live if you were not there beside me? If we are to join your mother and Spencer, then that will be. If there is no time to sing together the Dirge of un-being then we will sing it together in the beyond."

I kissed her tears and held her close, promising that come what may, I would not leave her on her own.

I let her fingers go, then sent my mind up to my Spellbinder and ordered Polonius and Barathon to drop down and take on board their cousins. I had spoken to them and had insisted that they do as I commanded. A great shadow fell over the settlement as my faithful ship hovered above us and dropped a transfer tube to take my grandchildren inside. We gave them all our blessings and insisted that they go back to the Spellbinder. They were now Ljo'sa'lfar in body and mind, but buried inside them were human genes that had emerged, giving them the gift of telekinesis and the ability to pass that talent on. The elfin race had benefited in the end from the mutation that had produced Molock and Eloen, but at an awful price. We had emerged stronger in the end and under my guidance a multi-sapient society had arisen. Now that the humans had an extended lifespan and the same telepathic powers as the elves, bestowed upon them by genetic engineering, they had become a different people.

My musings were interrupted by a familiar voice. "Long Shadow, we have decided to stand with you, Night Flower and I, in case we are needed."

"Sam! I ordered you back to the ship and safety! You and No'tt-mjool should be awaiting events in the Spellbinder, not here," I replied with concern.

"You are my High King," Sam replied, "and you brought me back from the dead to stand by your side. There is no other place I would rather be than with my King and friend. Night Flower is sure that she and I stand with you here when the Collective wakens. She still cannot see a space in the future that you are missing from. That goes for all of us here. Here is where we are meant to be, and I will not argue with that. All I can tell you is that something will happen that will change all of our lives. I would not miss it for the world!"

I stopped and stared at my half-human friend as he stood resolute before me. Like mine his hair was now silver and his skin colour was darker than my light brown, but his ears were as pointed as any elf. The only real difference between us was his lack of wings and his larger build. When I had resurrected him with my blood, I had infused elfin characteristics in him and all of my comrades who had assisted me in the rescue of Ameela. They were Halflings, neither elf nor human but the best of both. I loved them all.

Once again Sam Pitts had taken his place by our side, to stand or fall with me. I entered his mind and showed him as only telepathy can, "Thank you Sam."

I turned to No'tt-mjool and asked, "How long before it awakens?"

"We have until the morning when the sun is halfway across the sky, my Lord," she answered. "There is time enough for you to prepare and sleep well before you meet the destiny that you were born for."

That evening I sat with Ameela and stared up at the full moon, looking at the great scar where the asteroid had hit on this timeline. Evolution on this world had not had the kick that the other parallel worlds had suffered or gained, to wipe out the dinosaurs and leave the Earth to recover and allow the age of the mammals commence. Vinr's Earth had the same moon-scar as this one and my people had settled that world and called it Haven, as we did our home on it. There too the velociraptors had developed intelligence and tool-using abilities when we found them. They had become great allies to our fight against the Dokka'lfar and I had granted them a Spellbinder of their own to explore the Rifts. They had found this world so like their own that they had expected much, and had not expected to find the problem they had been landed with. They had the intelligence to do all the right things. Now it was left to me as High King to sort out the predicament that had presented itself.

"We should get some sleep before the morning dawns, my love," Ameela said, standing at the entrance to our temporary home. I too stood up and walked over to her and held her in my arms and buried my nose in her hair. She smelt of flowers freshly picked and her hair was soft, benefiting from the shower we had taken in the Spellbinder. Her lemon-coloured hair had turned to silver, as had mine over the centuries that we had lived together. We were both showing our age, although there would be some while yet before we would pass over. The regrowth of her feet and lower legs had taken a great toll upon Ameela's youthfulness, although the gift of life energy from the grandchildren had replenished much of it. Eloen had stolen a great deal of life energy to stay young, and that was against all elfin law. We had seen the awful truth when we had at last confronted her about how old she really was, before my son gave his life to restore her. She had stolen his soul, as well as his life and we still missed him as if it were yesterday.

That night we slept together naked and entwined in each other's arms, not knowing what the morning would bring when the Collective awoke. All we had was Night Flower's surety that she could not see a space in the future where we would stand.

My family slept uneasily in the Spellbinder far above us while our daughter Mia wrestled with the strange idea that if we were to be destroyed, then she would have to take on the task of High Queen and rule in our stead. My scientific friend, John Smith, could not doze but for a few moments at a time before the awesome task that he might be called upon to perform tormented his fitful sleep. Each Spellbinder commander had the same task of directing the Breath of the Sun at each target if called upon, with the knowledge that they had never done this before. All they had to do was to copy John Smith's trial-and-error method of controlling the Rifts. Each memory bank was fully charged with the method, but it still needed the mental power of controlling the opening and closing to carry it through. Holding the aperture at the bottom of the Rift to a narrow gap would require great restraint and concentration.

As the dawning sun lit up the settlement it found me ready and waiting. We had both washed and dressed in simple tunics and pants. Sam and No'tt-mjool were also awake. They had laid a breakfast of bread, smoked meat and fruit along with fresh water. I sent a wake-up call to all the Spellbinders fixed in their positions over the 'Trees' to get ready, although we had a few hours yet, according to my far-seeing troll. We had warned the velociraptors that the Voice that Tells would awaken this morning and to be ready for the alien to re-enter their minds.

Painfully slowly it seemed that the sun crawled ever upwards into the sky, until Night Flower called out, "It awakens soon!"

We stared at the dormant 'Tree' about a mile or more away to see it suddenly erupt into life and movement. It swayed from side to side and the leaves that had sprouted under the controlling mind's influence now angled themselves to catch all of the sun. The anchor roots stiffened and brought the swaying 'Tree' under control. Those of the velociraptors that carried the seeds of the Collective became very still and looked around at the settlement to regain some knowledge of what had transpired. They saw us sitting in front of the giant tortoise shell and froze.

I made the sign of empty hands.

"You gave me great pain," the Collective projected into my mind, sharing that moment with me.

"It was necessary that you be brought under control" I replied. "My intention at that time was to destroy you. You must have thought that likely, because you have scattered your static form all over this planet. I warn you that if you try to take over my mind, I have left instructions to destroy this world, along with those of us who have waited for you to awaken. You will cease to exist. This will automatically happen, leaving this world lifeless."

The Collective considered this statement and then replied, "I can understand your fears. Much has changed on this world since I came. I hid my form under the canopy, but in my absence it has become obvious to your people where each and every 'Tree' is situated. This is true, but I have time on my side. There are millions of my seeds scattered over this world, some carried by my hosts, some buried in the ground waiting for the right time to reproduce my static form. They could wait a million years before emerging, and by that time you will not be here."

"That leaves me with one alternative, and that is the total destruction of this world," I replied, "for my people will not willingly serve you and play host to your seeds. I will show you what happened when you wrested the control of the opened Rift from my Spellbinder and its master. "

I opened my mind and showed the Collective the swath of destruction that had swept across the lands, vaporising everything in its path, and reminded it that this was poised over every 'Tree,' just waiting for my command to be carried out.

A feeling of pure horror washed over me, not for the burning of the 'Tree' that had housed the central intelligence but the destruction of the land and the velociraptors that had served it. This was something I had not been expecting from this alien being. It had discovered the emotion of compassion.

The mind of the Collective turned to mine, and I was aware much more of how it had changed from parasite to symbiont during the time it had held sway here.

"You must not do this to this world. It has the right to live and evolve. Show me your worlds and your many different people that live within your power. Let me understand what it is to be you."

I considered the situation and made a decision. From what had leaked out during our 'conversation', this being was developing ethics. I opened my mind and urged Ameela to do the same, along with Sam Pitts and Night Flower. The history of what I had achieved, along with all of our struggles, lay bare for this alien organism to scrutinise.

My telepathic link to the Collective went quiet, as it considered the massive chunk of knowledge we had freely given to this new symbiotic life-form scrutinised it in depth.

Vinr-tat approached us and said, "The Voice that Tells has spoken to all of us that serve its needs. No harm must befall you and we are to help in any way we can. We are your people and you are our High King. We bring you food, that you may not hunger."

She motioned to the waiting raptors, who brought us pieces of roast meat set on large leaves with baskets of fruits and cooked roots. We had not realised just how hungry we had become and ate heartily of all that had been provided. I too had much to ponder, in that I had been inside the Collective's mind and could see what had been achieved here. I could also see what it intended for the future if left in control of the ecology. If only we could have some control over this alien, then it could be a force for stability and growth. If we destroyed the 'Trees', the Collective would still live in a diminished capacity through the seeds carried by the hosts, and long after we were all dead the buried seeds could re-emerge and take control over this world and then export its seeds through the Rifts throughout the parallel universes. No matter what, there were no easy options.

"High King, I would speak with you and explain my new situation. I am the sum total of the overlying intelligence of every velociraptor connected to me by hosting my seeds. Being here and building this telepathic link has created ME. Without them I would once more be a creature of instinct and become without any identity. I could become much more if others joined my rapport. I am the Collective, evolved to do just that and more. I have lived on many worlds that were barren of intelligence until I landed there. I do not want to sink into mindlessness. You do not trust me to avoid learning how to manipulate the Rifts and spreading my influence across your settled worlds.

"The solution is simple. Become me. I can sense that your

host grows weak and is soon to cease to function. All that you have built will be left in the hands of another, and you know that they are not ready. I say again, become me and we can share this world and all the other civilizations that are building their own futures. I offer you a state of near-immortality to continue to guide your people and protect them. I can blossom and spread your seeds through the Rifts to as many parallel Earths as it is possible to find. You will find that this organism that is part 'Tree' and part hosted seed is capable of doing much more than you could ever imagine."

I was stunned and shaken to the core of my being at what was on offer.

The Collective had persuaded me that its rule over the velociraptors would be beneficial and would last for eons. Together we would build a civilization on this world that would be peaceful and become part of the Elfin Commonwealth. As its sentience had grown, the old instincts of survival had been overcome by reason. The addition of myself into its consciousness added a safeguard into the equation.

Ameela dug her nails into my arms to get my attention and said, "Where you go, I go, Peterkin. If this is your destiny to do this thing, then it is mine to enter into this relationship along with you. You will not leave me here without you."

No'tt-mjool joined into our mind-set and said, "This is what I have seen. There is no space in the future that does not contain both of you."

Now I understood what Cailleach had meant when she had talked about the many paths I must tread and how I would have more than one struggle to overcome. There was also that fleeting feeling of awe that she had regarded me with before she vanished back into that other existence. Would I ever join her there along with all of my friends? I might never know.

CHAPTER FIFTEEN

I sent my mind up and away to every Spellbinder that was hovering within destructive range and told them all to stand down. They were now free to pursue their own agendas while I spent some little time in the skull of my old friend John Smith, removing the trigger I had set there. His feelings of relief still haunt me even now. Our sons and grandchildren were not happy about the change in our impending state, but accepted my insistence that this was not just a solution to a problem, but an incredible change of fortunes for us all.

I made our link with the Collective and asked, "What do we do now to join you?"

"Strip naked and fly towards the Tree that ministers to this settlement and approach me. I will reach out to you both and absorb you into my trunk and there you will achieve union with me," the alien replied.

Ameela and I disrobed and stretched out our wings to pull out all the creases, embraced each other and kissed for the last time. We launched ourselves into the air and climbed steadily upwards, catching any thermal that would assist. We could see the 'Tree' thrusting itself through the canopy, and glided towards it. As we approached the black trunk it opened and two long tentacles reached out to us. We felt the touch of the Collective as the tendril curled about our bodies and drew us into the hole. The edges closed over us and we lay in perfect darkness, side by side, being absorbed into the very fabric of the Collective.

Now Ameela and I were at one with the Collective, totally absorbed into its substance. Through the root system I could feel every life-form's mind and needs. Our group mind could now reach out to all the home worlds throughout the rifts, and we scattered our seeds. We were with our people on Haven and also on Alfheimr by materialising as living beings. Other worlds that had been settled by the commonwealth were all part of this mental union and could be guided by their High King and Queen from here. All of the instincts and powers of the Tree were ours to use and we had millions of years to understand all that we were capable of doing. We were already extracting metals from deep beneath the soil by transferring the particles through the root system. This would be exuded by a major root to wherever it was needed. This world could be exploited without polluting the skies or waterways. Networks of canals would be formed by our root systems to divert water to where it was required. In time cities would be built for the velociraptors that were indigenous to this world. Those who carried the dormant seeds would enjoy extended life until the time came to achieve a stationary situation, when they would root into the soil and become the mature stage of the growth that we enjoyed. All would be telepathically joined across the multiverse on every parallel Earth that became settled.

This would be a symbiotic relationship that would last until the stars themselves ran down. Just as elves with their long lifespans looked thousands of years into the future, the new Collective would now look billions of years ahead, and plan accordingly.

The End

ND - #0495 - 270225 - C0 - 229/152/17 - PB - 9781861512178 - Matt Lamination